Cuddling
WITH
CHUPACABRA

URBAN LEGEND EROTICA COLLECTION

Cuddling WITH CHUPACABRA

HONEY CUMMINGS

4 Horsemen
Publications, Inc.

4 Horsemen
Publications, Inc.

Published By: 4 Horsemen Publications, Inc.

4 Horsemen Publications, Inc.
PO Box 417
Sylva, NC 28779
4horsemenpublications.com
info@4horsemenpublications.com

Cover & Typesetting by Valerie Willis

Paperback ISBN-13: 978-1-64450-095-8
Audiobook ISBN-13: 978-1-64450-022-4
Ebook ISBN-13: 978-1-64450-020-0

Dedication

To Brandye
Thank you for helping me cook up a wild child
like Clara and a Sheriff to match!

XOXO
Honey Cummings

Table of Contents

1

THE BAD DIVORCE

*C*lara Worcestershire bit her lip, aroused. Her eyes scanned the text message, making her shift her hips in the driver seat. Pulling a lock of dirty-blonde hair from her ruby lips, she inhaled deep. She slid the seatbelt over, hating how it cut into her c-cup breasts and throat. Clara was the curvy, cute girl from next door and returning to her hometown filled her with memories of wild nights.

Oh, how I've missed partying after a good rodeo.

Daisy dukes, cowgirl boots, and shirts tied up to bare as much skin as possible were Friday night requirements. Bleach-blonde hair crowned her head, topping tanned skin and blue eyes; she never had a dull moment. Which meant helping a bull rider rock his pickup truck on occasion. Again, the arousal washed over her as she recalled her bachelorette party. Umber skin taut over muscles and eyes that glowed gold. Even now, the sensation of Jakob Regadera grinding against her made her

1

throb with want. She found herself back in the land of bronco and bull riding. The possibilities for real physical fun excited her.

A loud noise forced her from her reverie, an oncoming truck slamming on its horn.

Shit! She jerked the steering wheel. *I'm in the wrong lane!* She ran off the edge of the road before pulling it back onto the asphalt.

She didn't want to destroy the one decent thing she'd won in the divorce, the whole settlement a complete farce if she was being honest. Her cheating ex-that-shall-not-be-named husband had run off with anything of value, leaving her only a collection of junk from an old estate and the Mercedes she had almost wrecked.

The phone buzzed again, and she bit her lip, fighting the temptation.

I can't sext and drive, or my libido will get me killed.

She was sexting with a twenty-year-old college student. Age wasn't a factor for her husband when he chose to explore his secretary's pussy for fun. In fact, her replacement was her first female friend when they'd moved to the Big Apple. *We were friends, or so I thought.* Granted, she had never learned her age nor how long he'd been cheating on her.

She grabbed up the phone again, texting a naughty response because, *equality and all that shit.*

[Clara: I unzip my dress.]

[Tommy: I take off my shirt, licking my lips. <PICTURE>]

Up ahead, a gas station came into view. She wiggled in her seat, aroused by the pic of a bare muscled torso. She did need fuel, but she also needed some fun without wrecking into oncoming traffic. The old country store had a worn-out sign reading *Scruffy's Quik-e-mart*. Inside, it seemed Scruffy was trying to sell far too much with the tiny square footage.

"Gas station, convenient store, and bait shop?" Safely stopped at the pump, she reached for her phone again.

[Clara: I moan and my hand travels up your inner thigh to…]

[Tommy: My cock is growing hard]

A knock on her window made her jump, interrupting her reading. Annoyed, she rolled down her window.

"Hiya, Ma'am. You in need of a pit stop?" The older gentleman grinned at her. He had lost more teeth than he currently had.

What is this craziness? Since when do people just come up and speak to you?

She glanced at her phone and smirked. "Sure am."

The old man nodded, giving her a key attached to a wood block.

What the hell? Was he just waiting for a chick to swing in and piss?

She eyed the man as he walked to the back of her car. She popped the gas tank and took the key around to the side of the building, an arrow with *restrooms* guiding her way. She opened the dented metal door and locked it behind her. Her eyes took a moment to adjust to the green glow of the florescent lights. A cracked mirror was the only thing on the wall behind a small pedestal sink. Despite the cracked tiles and peeling paint, it was clean.

Finally, some privacy.

She looked down to finish writing the text she'd nearly died over.

[Clara: My dress falls to the ground.]

[Tommy: I lean down to suckle a nipple.]

[Clara: I grip the bulge in your jeans.]

Scrolling up, she pulled his picture back up on her phone, while she waited for his response. Humming, she took in all that tan skin and those hard planes. She didn't know his real name, just defaulted to Tommy, but she couldn't forget that body. Blue eyes and sandy-blonde hair, he was a dead ringer for a young Brad Pitt.

[Tommy: I bite your neck and fondle your breasts.]

A flash of provocative want washed over her again. How she wished it could be the real thing and not a virtual tease. But it was better than nothing. At least she knew what how it felt when a man could handle her body.

Reaching up, she fondled herself, twisting a nipple as she imagined him nibbling her neck. At last, she took her turn.

[Clara: I unzip your pants and take your thick, smooth dick in my hand.]

The thought just made her blood boil. A rush of youthful vitality had her reaching down the front of her own pants. Her breathing deepened, and she pushed her underwear aside, imagining a wild fantasy.

The phone buzzed.

[Tommy: Yes, baby. Stroke me.]

Her finger circled her throbbing arousal, praying for release. She slid her thumb to text her next desire. Her body hot with want. A moan escaped her.

[Clara: I run my tongue across...]

A loud knock landed on the bathroom door, startling her. The fantasy shattered.

Damn it.

She looked at the ceiling.

What do you have against me?

"Just need to use the bathroom." A lady's voice came through the door.

Shit, the door's that thin? Could she hear me?

"Just a minute." She flushed the toilet to reduce questions, then washed her hands.

When she opened the door and emerged, a woman with one child tucked under her arm, the other doing the potty dance, appeared. Clara held the door open for them; her cheeks flushed with guilt as she noticed the desperation on the little boy's face.

The lady hauled her two nagging children into the bathroom. "Much obliged," she said as Clara handed her the key.

The sight of them had flushed her fiery libido and sultry mood into the toilet. She sighed, opting for a drink instead. She exited the sexting session, bitter to abandon her fun. Checking her GPS app, she was only four miles shy of her destination. Taking a water from an iced barrel, she headed for the counter to pay.

An old woman gave her an appraising look. "You from out of town?"

Clara just nodded. She hadn't wanted to make this trip, and she didn't want to make it worse by explaining to strangers where she was going and why. After all, there's a reason why she'd escaped the small-town mentality. *Everyone's always up in your business... gossip city.*

"Where you headed?"

And there it is. Clara tapped her credit card on the counter. "Worcestershire Estate."

The old lady scanned her water. "Why the hell would you go there? It's cursed land. Nothing there but a barn and an old, abandoned house."

"Cursed?" Clara didn't remember hearing such rumors. *Is that why he wanted to leave it behind? Fucking dick. Giving me a haunted piece of shit.*

The old lady nodded. "Pump two, right?"

Clara nodded again.

The old lady punched in some numbers on the old register. "$48.23."

Sliding her card over, she asked again, "What do you mean by cursed?"

Swiping the card, the old lady gave her a long stare. "For generations, something evil has preyed on the cattle there, killing them in mysterious ways."

Clara laughed. *Why am I letting these hillbillies scare me with their silly superstitions?*

"She ain't kidding." The old man from earlier appeared, wiping his hands on an oily cloth.

Clara reclaimed her credit card and swiped the water bottle from the counter. Smirking, she gave him a skeptical expression, remembering the silly local urban legend she had ignored in favor of chasing boys and fuc...

"All the livestock dies from blood loss, sucked dry by that damn Chupacabra." He shoved the dirty rag into his overall pocket.

"Don't speak its name!" the old lady snapped, forming a cross over her chest.

"It's only fair to warn her about the shapeshifter," the old man defended. "Old man Baker claimed the beast could walk like a man when it turned."

Clara laughed. "Thank you, but I'm sure I'll be fine. I'm not the superstitious type."

The man gave a disapproving grunt.

As she stepped out the door and returned to the comfort of her car, she was glad to be back on the road, following the GPS. It won't be long before this disastrous trip was over. Thoughts of her cheating ex-husband, her sexting buddy, and the crazy superstitions intertwined her thoughts as she drove.

What kind of life have I made for myself?

The Family Curse

Sheriff Jakob Regadera sat in his patrol truck, glaring at himself in the mirror. Grabbing an old fast-food napkin from the seat, he wiped away blood from the corner of his mouth. He hated how he had lost control. Frowning, he put the aviator style sunglasses on, hoping they would temper his unpredictable ability. Being a Chupacabra shifter had its pros and cons. One look into his eyes, and he could charm the pants off any woman or man. Granted, he'd cheated the system, using his ability during investigations, but lately, there was no way to turn off the switch.

I can't believe what I did this morning. Turning up the CB Radio, he waited for the inevitable call. *Any minute, Mr. Baker will make a complaint. I'm shocked it's taking him this long.*

The full moon was only a few days ago. The new moon was his trigger, unnerving him. Last night, he had been monitoring local coyote activity when he felt the shift, abrupt and unnatural. He swallowed, still tasting the metallic tinge of blood on his tongue. Cracking open a Monster© energy drink, he guzzled it down, swishing the unwanted flavor from his mouth.

After gulping it down, he checked his teeth in the rearview. *Christ, I have fangs almost as long as a vampire's canines. What the hell is happening to me?*

Both his parents had been of Mexican descent, thus his umber tanned skin had been a blessing and curse. Dark black hair and a permanent five o'clock shadow on his chin and jaw-line made him rugged. He maintained a crewcut so he didn't have to stress about getting it caught in rope during his side gig as a bull rider. The rest of the small-town law enforcement were far from being as in shape as Jakob. His large biceps were tight in the sleeves, and even in an extra-large shirt, the buttons strained across his chest.

Every muscle is itching just to strip naked and run wild across the pasture.

"We have a situation down at Baker's Ranch. What's your 20 Sheriff Regadera?" The CB Radio crackled to life with a woman's voice and Jakob sighed.

He picked up the receiver and pinged back. "10-4. Grabbing donuts and energy drinks at Scruffy's Quik-e-Mart."

There was a giggle before she continued, "Coffee's better. Anyhow, Mr. Baker wants to file a report. Can you do an in-person report this morning?"

He took another sip of his drink and glanced at his fangs one more time. Dipping his sunglasses down, he groaned. His irises flashed yellow with reptilian slits for pupils. Blinking a few times, they faded back to brown, and he shoved the glasses back in place. For now, he wouldn't be taking them off in public. Cracking his neck, he watched as a trailer of bulls pulled in to fuel up.

His stomach growled with hunger. He could hear their hearts beating, the blood rushing in their veins, the taste...

"Did you copy, Regadera?" the radio screeched, bringing him back, and he cursed under his breath.

"10-4. Yeah. I'll go meet him at his house." Hanging the CB receiver on its hook he put the pickup in drive.

Licking his lips, he gave the cattle one last lingering look before ignoring his hunger. He was about a thirty-minute drive from the Baker's ranch, a fact he only knew since he'd just come from there after eating the livestock. Normally, the need to feed was stronger during the full moon. To curb the appetite, he'd buy a goat or two and set up shop in his barn so no one could see their fate.

They'd ask and he'd tell the half-truth; *I ate it.* Goat meat wasn't frowned upon, but what he didn't share is he'd had no desire for that part. Instead, he sucked them dry of their blood. During big events, he'd invest in a cow. Or an old mare fated for the glue factory.

But whatever happened last night, he wasn't prepared for, almost shifting the entire way.

Picking up his cell phone, he called his father. He hadn't spoken to him for years, but this wasn't the time to rage about the past. When his mother died, they'd gone separate ways, and he'd started a new life.

"Hello?" Jakob tensed at the sound of his father's heavy Mexican accent.

"Hey, Dad. It's JR."

There was silence. The last time he saw his father was after he'd eaten his father's prized Thoroughbred out of spite. He hated that the man gambled and worked the circuit. The way he treated those horses was damn near inhumane. And when that horse broke its two front legs, someone needed to put the poor thing out of its misery. His father was going to milk him dry for the semen and breeding stock.

"Look, I just need to know if there's someone that I can talk to about ... my condition." He inhaled deeply, holding his breath.

"You didn't seem worried about it when you ate Hercules."

There it is. Still pissed about the fucking half-dead horse.

"Fine. I'm sorry. I was young and reckless." It was an empty apology and they both knew it. "I'm having ... issues."

Another painful pause.

"Dad, I shifted last night," he confessed.

"How the hell did that happen?" The tone in his dad's voice quickly shifted to concern. "Were you caught? Do you need a place to hide?"

"N-no. I just need to talk to someone. See if this is ... normal." He struggled to get the last word out, shifting in the driver's seat. "I have fangs like a fucking vampire and my eyes won't stop shifting. It's bad."

"Jakob, your mom never really discussed the family curse." It was the worst news ever. "But what I do know, is that there are others out there. Shifters, that is. Find one and they might know something. I can do some digging on my end. Maybe there's something in her things."

"You still have her things?" His chest ached at the idea, *I thought he said he got rid of it all.*

Another pause. "Yeah. I kept it. Every piece."

Now's not the time to talk about that. Jakob took a left turn down an old clay road. "I've got to go. Let me know what you find."

"JR. Be careful."

He pushed end. Whether that was all his father had to say, he didn't want to know or hear that he loved him. There were still too many bitter memories drowning what few good ones lingered.

As the truck came around the bend, Mr. Baker stood waiting for him, a shotgun in hand, giving a mean stare.

Jakob cut the engine and pulled himself from the truck. "Morning, sir."

The old man spat tobacco at his feet. "Morning nothing!" he yelled, pointing his gun. "Something ate my goats, including old Bessie."

Jakob licked his teeth, recalling the flavor. "R-right. You want to show me where?"

"The barn, JR." Scoffed the old man, hobbling ahead of him. "Where else would they fucking be?"

Jakob rubbed the back of his neck. "Not everyone is as diligent as you are, old timer."

"Coyotes have been lurking along the fence line." He stopped, pointing at a trail of blood. "But this wasn't a coyote, JR. That's the work of the Chupacabra."

"Mr. Baker." Jakob inhaled deeply, enjoying the scent of blood in the air. "That's an urban legend. There's no such thing."

"I saw it," declared Mr. Baker, his voice shaking. "Some sort of lizard thing."

Paling, Jakob walked up to the old cow's body, squatting with his back turned to Mr. Baker. "I'm telling you, it's a myth. I was out here tracking a pack of coyotes or wild dogs. They must've found a way in the fence. Maybe they've got mange, makes their skin scaly."

"JR, that thing had yellow eyes and scales like a snake." Another splatter of chewing tobacco hit the ground behind him. "Squatted just like you are now. Just sucking her dry."

Jakob's heart quickened. "Is that so? Maybe it was a cougar?"

"No. No fur. Too big for even that," Mr. Baker muttered to himself.

Looking at the cow, he could see the fang marks he'd left on her jugular. He saw the whites of her eyes for a split second, but the charm of his golden eyes had calmed her. She laid down, willing as he sunk them in. Blood hot and thick, but he hadn't been satisfied with the two goats in the stall beside her. The flesh had been torn away, still attached. Guilt filled him. She bled out. He had aimed to take just enough to let her live, but when the old man swung open the barn doors and fired a warning shot, he ran.

"I'll put it in the report." He stood up. "Should I send someone to help you with the carcass?"

"Yeah," the old man said, then sighed deeply. "Look, JR. Just put down coyotes did it."

He swung back to the old man, confused. "Are you sure?"

"My sugar, you see. It was high when I checked it last night and again this morning." He rubbed his forehead and sat on a nearby haybale. "I don't know what I saw."

A weight of relief washed over Jakob. "I see. I'll send some folks over to help you clean this up. If your diabetes is acting up, might do you some good to rest and let someone else do the work. I'll pay. You've lost enough today."

"R-right." They met eyes and Jakob was thankful he had aviators to protect his secret. "You're right, Sheriff."

He patted Mr. Baker on the shoulder. "Maybe I can get you a new cow. Even a goat or two."

Mr. Baker shrugged, still glaring at his Bessie. "I won't say no to that either. Long as you set things right, I can't complain."

Making it back into his pickup, Jakob could breathe again. Another stolen look to the rearview made it clear his eyes were still golden. He was reaching for his cell phone when the CB radio cracked. Abandoning his aim, he turned it up and grabbed the receiver.

"Repeat that last message, Suzie. I just got back to my truck."

"There's smoke coming from the old Worcestershire Estate," she repeated. "Do you copy?"

"10-4." Jakob licked a fang and furrowed his brow. "I thought it was abandoned?"

"That's a negative." There was a pause, but he knew Suzie craved gossip. "Rumor is Clara's back in town and they're going through the big 'D', and I don't mean Dallas. And he got the palace and left her the shack."

Good lord, when was the last time I saw Clara? High school? No, her bachelorette party when... shit.

3

The Fuel

*C*lara had just turned on the radio to calm herself when her cell phone rang. Excited that it might be her sexting buddy still wanting to finish off live on the phone she answered too quickly.

"Hey," she said with excitement.

"You're late." Her ex's cold voice rumbled through the speakers.

Her body flooded with the wrong kind of warmth this time. Her pulse quickened with anger, and she retorted, "Which wouldn't have been an issue if you hadn't hidden half of my belongings in the middle of nowhere!"

"Don't make me call the sheriff. I doubt he'll tolerate your disrespect by wasting his time with your bullshit," he drawled.

"How considerate. I wish you gave that much consideration when you decided to *fuck* my best friend." She turned down a clay road, a broken sign saying Worcestershire leaning against a tree. "How dare I waste *your time*, because wasting ten years married to you was..."

Her ex gave an exaggerated sigh, just to ensure she heard over the line. "Don't be crass, Clara. Have some dignity. You've already lost the divorce. It'd be a shame to have you handcuffed in the backseat of the sheriff's car."

"Taking the high road now, are we?" she laughed. "Well, I'm on this road to this cursed farm of yours."

"Cursed?" She wouldn't have noticed the raised note in his voice as panic if she hadn't lived with the man for so damn long. "Who says it's cursed?"

His voice sounded defensive. *How odd.* "The locals."

"How foolish of you to believe local superstition."

There it was...

His defense mechanism. He'd used it before when she'd suspected him of the affair. At that point, he'd denied it before accusing her of some fault. It took a private investigator to uncover proof of his dirty deed, and even then, he'd accused her of causing him to cheat. She decided to push him, instead of just letting it go. It became a game, setting things up for the fun of it, sometimes out of curiosity. At the end, it ruined the divorce process, but she regretted nothing.

"Naïve enough to walk on a farm where a Chupacabra has been eating the livestock? Is that why it failed? You were sucking your cattle dry and ran the family business down like you did me and our marriage?" A grin came to her face; she could still play the games.

A nervous laugh came over the speaker. "No one would believe that," answered the sinister voice.

Concern drew her brow together as the wrought iron gate came into view. It leaned into the brush and overgrowth. There were no signs of anyone ever living there when she'd let him sweep her off to the city. She hadn't planned to be in

Gandersville for long, but she didn't have the money or means to go anywhere.

Was this some great divorce joke or something? What creepy hell was this?

"I'm here," she said, ending the call. He had started whatever snarky retort he had for her, and she smiled.

She stopped in the middle of the driveway and looked around. For miles, there were rolling hills of vibrant green grass and driveway asphalt that had become gray with wear. She got out of the car and a breeze caught her hair, the sun high in the sky. The crisp white paint was a stark contrast to the green lettering on the sign reading *Worcestershire Ranch*. It had lost its footing now, rust painting it as it leaned against the wrought iron gates. She could see buildings at the end of the long drive, leading to the farm. It didn't feel creepy. Under different circumstances, she might even appreciate the country more, living in a place like this had she visited it in its prime.

Her phone buzzed with a new message.

[Tommy: Did I lose your interest? Lol]

She decided not to respond. Eventually, she'd provide an excuse later, but now, she was distracted. Like it or not, this is where life had landed her, and it was time to collect her shit.

She got back in the car and drove up the remainder of the drive. It was surprisingly well kept past the neglected gate and got closer to the antique farmhouse.

Shutting off the ignition, she stepped out and took it all in. There was no one in sight. She walked up to the porch and knocked on the door. No answer.

These country folk ... they're probably out hunting right now.

"Hello?" she yelled out to no one in particular.

She walked around the house; it was in decent shape. If her ex hadn't owned the property, she would have loved it even more. Making her way back to the front, she saw a large van driving up the long road. *The movers were late too.* The truck rumbled up and backed up to the porch steps. Clara crossed her arms, tapping her foot with annoyance. A frail elderly man got out of the cab, followed by three lanky college boys.

He nodded his head to her. "Ma'am."

"Hey." She managed a smile. "I guess we're just waiting on the sheriff?"

"Not unless you plan on giving us a hard time." The old man nodded at her and waved on the motley crew. "These boys will make quick work of it. We'll be out of your hair in no time."

The three college boys reminded her of everything she had left behind in Gandersville: youth and a carefree sex life. The tallest figure moved closer, smiling, reminding her of the picture she'd received from her sexting buddy. He had sandy-blonde hair and a worn-out band shirt. With huge broad shoulders, he wasn't overly bulky but lean and muscular. Her libido kicked into high gear, loving the confidence of his movements and the possibility of other rhythmic activities.

As he came closer, he had a face to match. *He should be on the cover of GQ, not out here in the sticks. Adonis incarnate!*

"What are you boys planning to take from this rundown shithole?" she asked.

The old man snorted. "We got a list from Mr. Worcestershire. We plan on taking just what's there, nothing more, nothing less. Court ordered. If you got a problem with it, you'll have to take it up with the judge."

She was ready to chastise the old man when the hunk's eyes met hers. Sparkling blue eyes memorized her, making her flush with excitement. His gaze roamed her face like a soft caress, and she yearned to have him touch her in all the right places. As he came closer, she could see the strong set of his jaw and the high cheek bones.

She bit her lip. *I wonder how chiseled he is under that shirt and jeans. I'd be more than happy to check for myself.*

"Mrs. Worcestershire?" said a soothing voice.

"Ms. Williams, actually," she amended. It had cost good money to regain her maiden name. "But call me Clara."

A smile spread across his handsome face, revealing a row of perfect white teeth. *Why the hell am I noticing his teeth? What's wrong with me?*

"Thank you for meeting me here...?" Her voice trailed, prying for a name.

"You can call me Trevor," he said. "Just a moment, I'll get the order and we'll begin. I'll still need your signature for this."

As he walked to the van, Clara got the most amazing view of his backside. Long lean legs, no doubt toned thighs. He grabbed a clipboard from the passenger side, nodding to the old man. The men made small talk, but Clara's thoughts were far away.

How can I get a man like that? Sexting and phone sex are a thrill, but to have a chiseled body on top of me, no under me, would be nothing short of amazing. Hearing her ex's name in their conversation brought on flashes of the divorce. She scowled, the tidal wave of emotions drowning her confidence. *I should definitely stick to phone sex. Jumping strangers while reclaiming my ex's portion of the divorce settlement is inappropriate. Right?*

Trevor's form filled the door frame as he walked into the house. Spinning back to her, he leaned against the frame, cocking his head. She shook the thoughts from her mind, mustering an empty smile.

He lifted an eyebrow. "You want to check the list with me? I want to ensure we don't leave anything behind."

Clara struggled to focus on his face, instead of drifting down his frame. "Sure, just let me get my list out of the car."

Ugh, I'm making a fool of myself.

Walking back to her car, she jerked the passenger door open and shuffled through her glove compartment. She had shoved her list from the lawyer there but had forgotten to review it.

The envelope was still sealed. *Well, I have to open it now.*

She tore into it, earning a nice paper cut. *Great.* Unfolding the paper, she looked over the list. Then, she saw at the bottom what clearly was her husband's contribution.

Taking anything other than what's listed will be seen as larceny and Ms. Williams will be prosecuted.

> The man knew she was on a warpath and had every right to fear he wouldn't get his way if she had a say.

What an asshole.

She looked at her reflection in the rearview mirror. Clara wasn't unattractive and everything was still in perfect working order. He couldn't satisfy her in bed, unable to keep up with her sex drive. At the end of the marriage, he had turned to her ex-best friend.

Who cares if I make a fool of myself! It's not against the law to flirt my way through this debacle. Not like I ever have to see him again anyway.

She contemplated a moment more, then shrugged out of her button up shirt. With only a white tank top on, she showed just the right amount of cleavage to remain publicly appropriate. Prepped and preened, she grabbed the list and walked inside. The interior of the house was cool and dark. Dust-covered drapes and boxes filled the rooms. It was more of a storage house than a livable home. She heard the men speaking from farther into the house. There was dragging and shuffling. The movers weren't wasting any time.

She caught up with them at the end of a long hallway that opened to a giant country kitchen, where the three young men were pulling some boxes out. Not a single glance came her way. Heat hit her cheeks, she glared at the list and decided it wasn't worth arguing over it. Everything was covered in dust, left here to rot like her.

Exploring the rest of the house was like walking on a country western set. The kitchen was enormous and the stairs creaking like hell under her feet. There were only two bathrooms, the one downstairs broken, and the one upstairs had an ancient clawfoot tub.

By the time she came back downstairs, the movers had emptied everything, leaving behind broken knickknacks and a button-tufted leather loveseat. She had lost sight of the handsome blonde hunk, and the old man approached her, muttering as he read his copy of the list. Clearing his throat, he earned an annoyed look from Clara.

"Ms. Williamson." He narrowed his eyes. "We don't have room for the loveseat."

"Not my problem," she scoffed.

"He's sending a company out to crate and ship it to him." He lifted an eyebrow. "Unless you intend to damage it. We've taken pictures so..."

Clara tilted her head back, staring at the brown popcorn ceiling. "Are you kidding me?" she said in disbelief. "Look, just leave. I won't touch the damn thing."

He nodded, scribbling on the paper and making her sign it as well. She followed him out, but *Trevor* had closed the back of the van and loaded in with the rest of the crew. Clara felt cheated. First her sexting, now Trevor escaping.

I just want to fuck someone.

She watched them leave, frowning. Looking back to the rest of the junk, a devilish idea came to mind.

They never said I couldn't burn his shit.

4
The Fire

Jakob sat in his truck, debating on reasons why Clara had returned. Worse, he'd been using the old ranch as a dumping ground for years. When George Worcestershire and his dad pissed him off, he'd done more than dump carcasses there. He single-handedly ate the bulk of the livestock and drove the rancher's living into the ground. That's what they deserved for the time when the Worcestershires beat him half dead.

They're a shit family, and when Clara still married that asshole...

A shudder rattled him. He could still taste her lips. The hunger for blood was almost insatiable as he covered his mouth. Goosebumps rolled across his skin. For the first time ever, he had a thirst for human blood. Picking up the CB receiver, he prodded Suzie for more answers or to at least pry the last of the gossip from her.

"Why call me and not the fire department?" He held his breath, burying his lust and hunger by pure force of will. "You did say it's a fire."

"Well, George Worcestershire called it in." Suzie sounded smitten with the man. "And he's harmless."

Sour memories boiled up, and Jakob's jaw muscles tensed. What the town didn't know, didn't see, was that Jakob worked on the Worcestershire Ranch as a farmhand. The pay was decent, but he'd wanted out from under George's dad in the worst kind of way. Rumors in town were building after Hercules had been sucked dry. Old superstitions took hold as they'd laid his mother in the ground. Word had gotten out. The Chupacabra was back in Gandersville.

This put him under a lot of pressure. With that, came his temper.

"George called? When did he return to town?" He put the truck in reverse, his curiosity piquing. "And why call me in?"

"Well, he comes and visits his mama in the nursing home once or twice a year." Suzie was settling into the conversation now; he had hit the jackpot. "Anyhow, he had no idea you were sheriff now. Seemed a little taken back by the news."

Jakob smirked, clunking the pickup into drive, retracing his route. "So, did he sell the old place finally?"

"Well, not exactly." After a moment, Suzie whispered over the radio, "You see, Clara lost big time in the divorce. It was ugly as sin, I hear."

Catching a glimpse of gold irises in the rearview, Jakob pushed the aviators up on his nose. "Okay, but what does that have to do with the old Worcestershire Ranch estate?"

"George is being generous. He's giving it to Clara."

Jakob snorted his drink out, choking on the energy drink.

"But she's a mess. Her crazy's showing," Suzie declared. "He's got things he wants out of there before she steps foot in the place."

Jakob could see signs of a fire as he started down a new clay road. "And what does this have to do with me going instead of the fire department?"

"He said that…" she lowered her voice, "crazy bitch," clearing her throat she finished, "set his stuff ablaze in the front yard."

Jakob started to laugh, stopping the truck on the empty road. "As we speak, she's burning her ex-husband's shit in the yard?"

"Oh yes! Terrible, isn't it?" Suzie was sincerely upset by the news.

"Oh, it's terrible all right." He couldn't hide his amusement.

"You better be on your way Sheriff Regadera."

"Almost there. Going as fast as I can, Suzie. Promise." Jakob put the truck in park and leaned back.

"You're such a good sheriff!"

He rolled his eyes, leaning his seat back and tilting his cowboy hat forward. Glancing at his wristwatch, he figured another thirty minutes or so should be enough to do some good damage. His mind wandered, unsettled by last night and even the surge of hunger the cattle had brought. Huffing, he tilted his seat back in place, annoyed.

That was short-lived.

Leaning on the steering wheel, he glared down the road, remembering how many times he had driven this way to work, or snuck in through the patch of trees and underbrush. His skin prickled. As he recalled the past, his last hours with Clara had always been bittersweet. His jaw twitched, remembering how her silky breasts had felt under his calloused hands. Glancing at his hands, he saw he'd lost those calluses years ago.

She used to bitch about how they felt like sandpaper, but it never stopped her from moaning.

Taking in a deep inhale, he could almost smell her perfume again. She was an animal that night of her Bachelorette party. They had shown up at the local bar where he and his bull riding compadres would end their nights. Across the room, he'd locked eyes with her. He had come looking for her, and she had come looking for him.

So blue, like a clear summer day.

He leaned back in his seat and pulled off his sunglasses. Glancing in the side mirror, he snorted at his yellow eyes. A smile came to his face, and he closed his eyes, thinking back to how she'd moaned and clawed at his back. It had been the first time he'd lain with someone who could keep up with his stamina. His eyes had shifted against his will, despite it being a full moon. The way she rocked against him, hungry for him to go deeper. She was all legs, her hair spilled in a curly heap, makeup smearing her beautiful face.

"Fuck me harder..."

Chills rattled him, making his shoulders shudder. He could still hear her haunting words. Looking back, it was as if she were giving him the last taste of her sexual freedom. Jakob inhaled deeply, shifting in his seat.

"Swallow me up, Jakob! I don't ever want to forget tonight..."

The craving for blood hit him like a tidal wave, tantalizing his arousal. His breath caught, and he shook his head, muttering a curse. Something about her drove him crazy back then, even now. The Chupacabra side of him could be sated, feeding on her. Though the idea of taking up the habits of a vampire disgusted him. It wasn't something his kind did out of affection. Plenty of times he'd noticed his father with a bandage on the neck with a smirk on his face.

She had started on top, the girl riding the bull rider.

He covered his mouth, running a tongue over a sharp fang. Now, his memories were returning. He bit her that night. Licked at her neck like a hungry animal and she had reacted with unadulterated passion. Nails ripped open his skin, her voice pleading for more. Jakob shifted, rubbing, shaking free of his memories.

I can't believe just thinking about it makes me this hard.

Groaning, he covered the golden eyes up once more, caving to his curiosity. Pulling the truck onto the road, he crept along. He could see the smoke plume coming closer. All he knew was the fuck of his life was back in town, angry over her divorce, and had left him for his worst enemy. He steeled himself.

I wonder how much she's changed. They've been married for what, ten years? Didn't make it too far. Shit, is that house even holding together enough for anyone to live in?

He turned the bend, pulling past the wrought iron gate. Stopping the truck, he stared at the scene before him. Blinking for a few minutes, he sat staring in disbelief. Flames shot up from the ground, towering over Clara and billowing black, acrid smoke. She threw out her arm, screaming on a cell phone before throwing it across the yard. Spinning on her heel, she locked eyes with him and froze. Her blue eyes coaxed him to tip his sunglasses down as she put her hands on her hips.

The thick lips scowled at him, her gaze measuring, before flicking him the bird. "Tell my ex-husband he can keep this shit pile. I'd rather spend the night in the jailhouse again."

He smirked at the declaration. She hadn't realized who he was yet, and he was glad. *There's no more of that desperate high school girl glow.* There before him, he saw a hungry woman who could kill a man with her libido. Goosebumps rolled over him, the scent of her perfume drifting on the breeze, just as always.

Gucci... Flora, was it?

Turning, she marched away in her tight jeans. Her hips swayed and he licked his lips. Looking to the burning pile, he recognized a few Worcestershire family photo frames, a painting, the old drapes, and... *Is that her wedding dress?*

Flipping a switch on the radio, he blurted over the megaphone, "You can't burn his shit in the yard, Clara."

She froze, staring at the truck in disbelief.

She's every bit as drop dead gorgeous now as she was back then. And those eyes are so hungry for... Christ, I'm so fucked.

5

EVERYTHING'S WET

Clara couldn't move. Those golden eyes, peeking at her over a pair of aviators, were a memory of the past. The last time she'd seen eyes like that, it had belonged to Jakob, a local bull rider who had a reputation for the wildest rides, in the ring and in the bed.

She blinked. *Don't tell me the sheriff is...*

Jakob stepped out of the truck, a receiver in his hand.

Fuck.

He leaned on the open car door and smirked. "Glad you remember me."

Anger and lust burned through her as she remarked, "Glad you remember my name."

His head slumped in defeat. Tossing the receiver in the truck, he slammed the door and headed toward her. The man walked with the graceful stride of some ancient predator that sent a shiver down Clara's spine—a mixture of fear and excitement. A part of her wanted to run, but those golden eyes under the dark lenses held her in place. She never took Jakob as a uniform man but seeing him now, again, took her breath away, rendering her mute.

What is it about those eyes that makes me useless?

He walked past her, breaking her glare. She followed him. He still had a slight limp; no telling if he'd gotten it in a one of the bar fights or bull rides. It reminded her of how he'd stalked across the bar, to *her*, that night at her bachelorette party. She already knew, under that sheriff's uniform, he had a chiseled body that she still ached to touch, just one more time.

I wonder if someone finally tamed the biggest bull in town. Oh? He has no rings on those fingers. He's fair game.

Clara crossed her arms, boosting her girls high enough to reveal some of the red lacy bra underneath. Smiling, she prepared for that moment he would turn and see her. Jakob squatted, turning on the hose bib. He was broader, more seasoned, and something about him made her blood rush. At last, he stood and turned, faltering in his steps. She bit her lips.

"Why are you looking at me like that?" he swallowed and shoved his glasses up. "You look like a hungry cougar ready to strike."

"So, what did you do after that night?" She would play dirty by bringing up the past as long as she got some fun before sundown.

Gripping the kink in the hose tight, he steeled himself. "I thought you'd forgotten something like that."

He feels it too; After all these years, the tension still remains.

"How could a girl forget a night like that?" She shrugged, following him to the fire. "My ex was never that good with his hands anyhow."

Spraying the fire, he grunted at the comment. The fire sizzled, the smoke thickening. Each item fell apart as the stream of water slammed into it. Clara walked closer and Jakob tensed. She grinned at the reaction, seeing an opening to make a move.

I'm about to fuck the sheriff!

Her hands glided across his torso, stopping right above his chiseled abs. The uniform did nothing to hide the herculean body underneath. She nestled herself into his back, the heat of his body tantalizing. He froze, still spraying water on the remains of her fire. Her hands glided up, curious at how far he'd let her go.

Is Jakob still every bit as wild as he was back then? Oh, this beats the sexting and movers hands down. I might get some physical loving after all.

She found the top button and loosened it. He did nothing to stop her as he continued to extinguish the stubborn flames. Another button undone, and his skin warm under her palm as she slid down his chest. She continued to unbutton his uniform, her other hand floating over ripples of muscles. He turned and blasted her with the water hose.

"Christ, do I have to put two fires out!"

Clara's white tank top was practically translucent as she sputtered, "What the hell was that for?"

"I could ask you the same thing!" Jakob dropped the hose, startled. "Stop it."

"No, the hell you didn't." She rung her hair out while glaring at him.

"I..." He stopped as if bewildered by his lack of action.

"Ugh, I needed a shower anyhow." Clara shed the tank top, wringing it out as she marched to the house. "Unless you plan on arresting me, this conversation is over."

"W-wait, you can't just strip naked in broad daylight." He gave chase.

"The hell I can't." She shoved through the front door. "It's my fucking house and property. All but that piece of shit furniture." She motioned at a leather loveseat.

"Clara, what just happened out there, it was..." She started up the stairs, and he grabbed her arm. "Look, I'm not going to lie. I was shocked to hear you were back. And yeah, I didn't forget that night. I couldn't forget that night."

She looked down at his hand, hot against her wrist, and raised an eyebrow. "Being rather physical, Sheriff. What do you plan on doing now that you have me in your grip?"

He tossed his glasses off, those golden eyes jolting her. With a yank, she fell onto him, and they locked lips. Their kiss deepened, increasing their passion. Clara wrapped her arms around his neck, coaxing his tongue into her mouth and began suckling it. The heat of a hand slid over her hip and into the back of her jeans, gripping her ass. She moaned, leaning all her weight into him, but it did nothing to budge him from the bottom of the steps.

Pulling free, she searched his face. "What made you change your mind?"

He smirked. "I could never refuse you when you're wet and ready."

She laughed, changing direction as she peppered his body with kisses. His hands gripped the railing as she untucked his shirt and began unbuttoning. She swore he'd earned a few new scars since the last time she'd explored him. Her fingers grabbed his belt buckle, the fabric tight.

I'm about to fuck the sheriff. How much hotter could this get?

Sitting on a step, she released the pressure, pressing down on his hard-on. He exhaled in relief. With a smirk, she began stroking his long cock. He leaned forward, pressing himself into her rubbing palm. Her body was on fire, throbbing to have him inside her. Memories of that night appeared in the present, and she wanted to have it all over again.

I don't think I ever found a dick bigger than this.

Her lips wrapped around the tip of his cock, twirling the tip as a tease. She unbuttoned her jeans and dove her hand under her panties. Staring up at him with her sky-blue eyes, she thought he glared down like a hungry lion. He rocked his hips, coaxing her to take all of him between her lips. She countered, licking the base to the tip, then continued to suckle. Clara began stroking herself faster, humming on his dick as she grew wet. He moaned, releasing a growl of frustration.

The wooden railing splintered under his grip; the golden eyes glowing.

Clara let him in, the hardened length glided across her tongue. Her fingers dove into her slick pussy, drawing the wetness toward her swollen clit. Circling, she was vigorous and desperate to come from hours of sexual frustration. His breath caught, and he purred as his cock pressed the back of her throat. She tightened her lips around his throbbing erection, rubbing her tongue against the underbelly. Jakob began rocking faster, enjoying the wet heat of her mouth and the power of her suckling.

Good lord. I can't fit the whole thing down my throat. I'm fucked if her tries to deep throat...

The wood creaked and she closed her eyes tight. He grew harder, her lips aching from the increased girth. She was enjoying this, having him at her mercy. This was something new, something they had never tried in the past, after all these years.

Is he going to break the railing?

A moan erupted, his cock pushing deep into her throat. She shook her head, unable to take him any deeper and he released. Throbbing, hot liquid filled her, and she swallowed, silently cursing. He had come like Mt. Everest, fast, hard, and unexpected. Her pussy ached, and she wanted more. Sweat poured from his chiseled chest.

Shit. I just gave the sheriff a free blow job, and I'm left here wet and hung out to dry.

She pulled away, unable to hide her frown as the bitter thoughts consumed her. Swallowing the last of the sweet cum, she wiped her mouth. Too terrified to look up.

You're dreaming again, Clara. This isn't the hungry bull rider from before. Just two adults clinging to one last good time.

THE NEED TO FEED

What the hell am I doing?

Jakob panted, assessing his moment of unrestraint lust. His fingers had dug into the wooden rails, and his eyes had yet to revert to their human form. When she placed her lips on his cock, he forced himself to remain still.

At last, he peered down, her look of disappointment rattled him. The Chupacabra side of him could smell it, how close she'd been to coming.

She wiped her mouth, refusing to meet his gaze.

Did I charm her into this? No, she had her hungry paws on me first and I was too afraid to look at her after snaring her from the car even with the glasses on.

He inhaled deeply. "Bend over," he demanded.

"W-what?" She turned and looked at him. His eyes were firmly shut. *I don't want her charmed. I want her ecstasy to be real, not a byproduct of the curse.*

"Turn around. I'm not done." He heard her shuffle.

"Jakob, look you don't..." Peeking, she had done so, unable to meet his gaze.

He reached out and jerked her jeans down off her ass. He sucked on his cheek, marveling at how her curvy hips hadn't changed. Sliding his hands over them, he dove between her thighs, fingers sinking into the throbbing heat. She moaned, leaning back into him, letting him probe her deeper. He licked a fang. His heart raced and the lust rattling through him began to rise.

Despite coming, he hadn't lost his hard-on nor the want to continue to pleasure himself inside her, anywhere she'd allow him to enter. They both moaned as he pressed his cock against her pussy, sliding faster than he had initially aimed to do. *She's so slick. Did she really get this work up sucking my cock? Christ, Clara...*

He grabbed the steps above her, her curves cupping up against him, the heat of their bodies waving into one another. Something about the sweat beading on her skin and the red bra enticed his hunger. Grinding hard and deep, ever faster as she gasped in her rising pleasure. He could feel how she tightened her legs, shaking until her orgasm peaked.

Jakob bit his lip, fighting the urge to taste her blood.

A scream released, her back arching.

Scream louder until...

Jakob saw his clawed hand and panicked. He pulled away, leaving Clara to finish her orgasm on the stairs, alone. He had been to this house plenty of times, so he knew where to dodge into the downstairs bathroom before she noticed his appearance. Locking the door, he glared wildly at himself in the cracked mirror. His golden, slitted eyes contrasted against the rising blue-gray scales speckling his chest.

Was I mid-shift again? And that thirst! Really? Old Bessie didn't do the trick this morning, fuck!

The cold knob snapped off as he turned it. "Shit!"

Knocks pounded on the door. "Jakob? Is everything okay?"

He ignored her, this time turning the hot water knob. "Son of a bitch!" he shouted as scalding water sprayed him from the faucet's base.

"Look. I know I came off aggressive," Clara said, sounding unsure of herself.

Reaching down, he splashed water on his face, praying it would invoke his features to change. He stared at his reflection in the mirror, at the water dripping from his chin. His eyes were fading to brown, scales retreating and normalcy was coming across his entire being. He leaned on the sink basin, getting a closer look at his eyes. It tilted, then cracked, shattering against the floor.

"Dammit!" Rushing, he turned the hot water knob off and it snapped, water spraying everywhere. "Mother fucking..."

He crouched, slowly shutting the water valve closed. Clara was wiggling the knob, banging at the door, and screeching his name. He glared at the old sink and the water flooding the broken tiled floor. *I can't believe they let this house go to tatters.* The thought made his chest swell.

Another wave of beating on the door brought him to the present, to the other mess awaiting him. He stood, inhaling deeply as he swung open the door.

Clara stumbled forward, her feet splashing into the flood. "What the hell happened?"

"About that..." Jakob glanced back at the mirror. *Good, eyes are still normal!* "I broke some shit, but I'll come fix it."

"I..." She took a step back, paling. "Look, I shouldn't have thrown myself on you. This divorce has made me depressed. I thought, if I fucked someone, I'd feel somewhat better about myself."

"Wait, what?" Jakob scrunched his face, confused. "I'm cussing because I broke your shit." *Not because we fucked.*

He started to laugh, then paled when he realized the pure devastation on her face.

"Clara..." he said, his heart skipping a beat. "No! No, no, I wanted that, I seriously was trying to, to..." *Shit! What do I say now? I couldn't admit I was shifting into a fucking Chupacabra?*

"Wait, your eyes." She squinted at him. "They're brown. But weren't they yellow before? Do you wear contacts?"

"YES." The lie left his mouth before he could think it through.

Clara took a minute, assessing her disheveled bathroom. "And the sink broke, how?"

"I had to remove my contacts." His mind raced flailing to grasp onto anything.

"They must've been hurting you when you ran away." She gave him a suspicious glare.

"Killing me."

"Ok, but I don't think..."

The mirror broke loose and scattered across the floor into tiny shards. Jakob cringed, watching the place fall apart around him. Clara shuddered, her skin dimpling. Jakob didn't flinch. Unlike her, he'd heard the moment the glue loosened from the drywall. He stepped out and shut the bathroom door behind him. He felt awkward, towering over her with his uniform laid open and jeans still unbuttoned.

She shivered again, and he wrapped his arms around her reflexively.

"Careful using the upstairs one. It may be in disrepair, too." She nodded her head; her body still damp from the hose earlier. "And I need to return to work. I didn't mean for this to happen, so just forget about it."

"Wait, what?" Clara shoved herself out of his arms, her eyes fiery. "You're just going to fuck me, break my shit, then leave?"

"I said I'd be back to fix it." Jakob now remembered how hotheaded they both could be as the tone in their voices grew stern. "I showed up to extinguish a fire."

"Great job, Jakob," she drawled. "You put my wedding dress out and my pussy."

His brow dropped low as he glared at her. "Now that you're back, stay out of trouble."

"Oh? Is that a threat?" As she crossed her arms, his eyes unwillingly fell to her cleavage.

"I'm leaving." He turned, buttoning his shirt with each stride. "I won't hesitate to put you in the containment cell if you act out, Clara."

"You can't cage me!" she flared, hissing like a feral animal.

The fresh air and sun hit him as he exited the house. He could breathe again, tucking his shirt into place as he glided past the smoldering debris. By the time he made it back to the truck, he paused to look at the front door. Part of him had hoped to see her there, glaring at him. Anything.

But she wasn't. *Good.* The thought was a mixture of pain and relief. *I don't need to rekindle something I didn't have in the first place.*

Swallowing, he got in the truck and started the ignition. He reached into his shirt pocket. Empty. Twisting and turning, he searched the bench seat, then the floorboard, patting the entire place, hoping to find what he needed. *My glasses.*

"Where the hell are my glasses?" he muttered.

"Here." She tapped on the window, startling him. "Lookin' for these?" She held up his aviators, and he rolled the window down.

"Y-yeah. Thanks. I need to put a bell on your neck. Not anyone can sneak up on me like that, you know."

Leaning in, Clara seemed calmer, despite still only wearing a red bra. "We were both releasing some pent-up sexual tension.

I get it. Sorry. I was quick to blow up about this being a tempo-rary one-off deal. It's been a shitty day. All and all, it was good to see you again, Jakob." She smirked. "All of you, that is."

He laughed, sliding on the aviators. "I suppose I've had a shitty day too."

She pulled away like a cat who caught the canary.

Let's hope we don't cross paths again. I don't think I could have stopped if it weren't for that untimely shift.

7

The Rodeo

Clara had her hands on her hips, picking herself apart in the mirror. It had been a long time since she wore a getup like this: cowgirl boots, jean skirt, and a bikini top hidden under a tied sleeveless flannel. This was topped only by her seagrass cowgirl hat with a silver and turquoise decorated leather band. She had found it in an abandoned box from her last days in Gandersville. Some part of her still felt defeated, leaving a place only to be dragged back.

"Girl, turn that frown upside down." Brandye nudged her before adjusting her girls in her own bra. "We got some cowboys to herd."

"I don't know, Brandye," Clara sighed, sitting on her friend's bed. "It's been a long time since I wrangled a cowboy."

"Oh c'mon. You know what they say?" She pulled Clara off the bed, and they started out the door to the old pickup.

"What do they say?" Clara climbed in through the creaking passenger door and slammed it shut. "Don't leave me hanging, Brandye-wine."

"Save a horse." She winked, bringing the truck into a roaring rumble. "Ride a cowboy."

They laughed.

The old truck bounced and hummed its way through the small neighborhood before finding its way to the two-lane countryside highway. Clara stared aimlessly at the passing fields and cattle. Unlike the city, it was boring and lacked all the finesse. Worse, she couldn't disappear into the crowds or hide in a café from gawking eyes.

"Clara, you alright girl?" Brandye glanced over at her. "You've been quiet, too quiet. In fact, I'm still salty about you not letting me know you returned to town weeks ago. I had to hear it from Suzie's mouth at the grocery store. Lord, that woman loves to gossip."

"Sorry, I just..." Clara's shoulders slumped, and she caught her exhausted face in the mirror. "I feel old and used up."

"Well, that's why we're headed to the rodeo." She nudged her arm. "Plenty of eye candy and prospects to rustle in the hay. You're a single woman again! Let's find you someone to fuck!"

Clara's face flushed. Her mind still savored the way Jakob had taken her on the stairs, the heat of his hands, the way... *No. Nope. I can't be falling for Jakob. Again. Falling for him is like dropping an anchor in this one-horse town.*

"Why are you blushing?" They were hitting traffic now with the rodeo stadium coming into view. "Don't tell me you hooked up with someone?"

"Maybe." Clara covered her mouth, hiding her smile. "It was just a quick hookup."

"And you're not going to tell me?" Brandye turned the old truck in the direction of where the parking guide had pointed. "Spill the beans, girl!"

"Nope. Last thing I want is for Suzie to tell half the town who I opened my legs for." Clara's brow furrowed as the truck pulled into a spot. "What does Suzie do?"

"She's the dispatcher at the sheriff's station." Brandye shuffled around for her purse. "You okay? You look like you're turning green on me."

Clara grabbed Brandye's purse from under her seat. "She works with ... the sheriff?"

"Yeah." She motioned for Clara to hand it over. "Hard to believe Jakob, the bull rider bad boy, would become the sheriff, right? I heard he was at your place because... wait a damn minute. Don't tell me you and the sheriff... again? Clara, you've got to be kidding me!"

Clara removed the flask of whiskey from Brandye's purse and shoved the green pocketbook toward her. "Not another word."

The liquor burned as she took a swig, wanting but failing to wash Jakob from her mind. Brandye took it back, taking her own gulp before returning it to her bag. The security guard waved them through the bag checker, giving them a wink as he ignored the flask.

They began walking around the staging area with stalls of horses and corrals of bulls and broncos. As far as one could see, Clara's eyes fell on young and seasoned bull riders of all kinds. Luckily, Brandye still had access since she'd gone from a barrel racer to Quarter Horse breeder.

The announcer blared across crackling speakers, "Next up is a real treat, a local favorite."

"Crap, we got here late," Brandye huffed, pulling Clara along to see the unfolding ride. "I swear he calls everyone a local favorite."

"He hasn't been here at Silver Spurs Rodeo for ten years."

Clara paled at the words. "Did he really quit after I left?"

"Who quit what?" Brandye and she found a spot at the railing so they could see the ring unobstructed.

A buzzer went off and a gate banged open. A black, angus bull launched out, a rider in headgear, jeans, long sleeve shirt on top, and a hand on the rope. The massive beast made the ground tremble under Clara's feet. Throwing a hand high, torso shifting to balance as the bull twisted under him with stunning speed, hind legs in the sky.

The rider looked like a jaguar clinging to its prey.

"Jakob," Clara whispered.

The timer flew, the golden eyes glinting under the mask. He lay against the slanted spine before rocking forward. Clara's body flushed with desire as she followed his movements. The bull spun and he started to slip. Again, the bull spun the other way, and Jakob lost his position on the bull's shoulders.

"That's our local sheriff! Ya'll, give him a shout!"

At that, Jakob shook his hand free. The bull rocked forward. Clara's breath caught. Horns were frighteningly close. Jakob's body twisted, dodging as he slid off. Landing on his feet, he ran for the closest gate and scrambled, up and over. He'd always been quick, like a cat landing on his feet. A strange calm came over the bull as if relieved the predator had left.

"Good Lord that man can ride," Brandye declared, pulling away from the gate. "C'mon Clara, let's go find some fun."

Clara followed, her eyes glancing at the fence one last time. He would be pulling off the helmet, sweat soaking his shirt. Jakob would shake off the long-sleeve flannel, grabbing a wifebeater or going bare. She bit her lip. This wasn't why she came, and he wouldn't know she was there like in the past, when they'd sneak off and...

Shaking her head, she cleared her mind of Jakob, instead focusing on the eye candy walking across their path.

Clara smirked. "Hey, cowboys."

It didn't take much to get their full attention. The two cowboys were lean and a little younger. Chaps, spurs, and cowboy hats only added to their sexy broad shoulders and chiseled jaws. Clara flashed a toothy grin, placing a hand on her hip. They returned the motion with their own smiles, relishing their full attention as the blue-eyed hotties took inventory of her body.

"What brings you to the rodeo today?" Clara lifted an eyebrow, the silver and gold belt buckles showing these boys had won at least first or second place at some point.

"Bronco riding. I thought you knew I rode now, Clara," the taller one replied, baffled. "I suppose it's been a while; I was still in the junior bareback division when you ran off and got married."

"Barrett?" Clara paled, glaring at Brandye.

Her friend was gasping for air, tears welling in her eyes as she laughed. "Did you just hit on my little brother?"

Face flushing, Clara bit her tongue. *I'm definitely too old to be hunting for ass in this place. How the hell did that goofy looking kid become so handsome?*

"I thought the bronco riding was still happening?" Brandye straightened herself again.

"Well, one of the bronco's broke a leg. They had to tranquilize the poor thing. They're waiting for the x-ray results to see if he's salvageable for breeding."

"Was the rider okay?" Brandye's fun had spoiled at the news. "The horse didn't roll over them?"

"I'm fine. Sprang an ankle trying to hop off and clear the way." Barret glanced at Clara, then back to his sister. "Are you guys back at it again? Aren't you a little old for that now? Paul will get jealous if..."

"Hush! I'm here for Clara, not me," she shushed.

"And you railed me about not saying anything." Clara crossed her arms. "Paul? Really? The guy from the neighboring ranch?"

"We both love horses?" Brandye shrugged, wincing at the heated glare.

Clara had heard enough. She spun on her heel, marching for the stalls. Not only was it the place to hook up, but a place she had come to resolve her past. This was the part she missed. The ability to go someplace quiet in an instant. Satisfied no one had chased after her, she slowed, she walked down the next lane. Concrete floors and steel I-beams held up the aluminum roofing overhead. Hay and sweet feed was a contrasting scent from the manure and sweat of the ring.

I'm stuck. I can't leave this place for some ungodly reason. All of this just reminds me of everything I failed to escape and... and... Jakob. I went with George to escape here, but I left him here and now...

She stopped, clenching her jaw, fighting her building anxiety. Tears were threatening to fall. Her chest ached. *I hate every part of why I'm here, back in this shitty cowpoke town. Who am I kidding?* Inhaling deep, she held it. She repeated this, calming her nerves. Regaining her composure, she began marching forward, aiming to walk it off. The animals were quiet. Last time she visited, the horses were eager to have their noses petted and checked her for treats. She swiveled her head, curious as to what on earth would cause the behavior.

The stall door swung open. Yellow eyes connected with hers, wide with equal surprise. Jakob rubbed a red line from his chin. Dread filled his face. Chills shook her body.

Is it wrong I feel happy to see him, even in my most vulnerable moments?

8

Rustle in the Hay

Standing over the horse, Jakob lost his appetite as the body started to grow cold. The poor thing had broken a leg mid-ride. In this industry, it was almost an instant death card. Being around all the livestock had added to the unusual hunger Jakob had been recently fighting. When the owner had pulled him to the side, the veterinarian had said there was no way to fix the leg. At that, they had turned to the local sheriff to put the animal down. The bronco had met him with calm, the jugular pulsing in his gaze. He couldn't say no to a personal favorite meal, and he'd taken his fill, lulling the horse to a peaceful death.

As he stormed out of the stall, he heard a yelp.

"Shit." Jakob's heart clenched, his belly warm with horse blood as he wiped his mouth. "Clara?" He slammed shut the stall behind him, hiding the dinner he had taken for himself. "Dammit, you need a bell or something."

Clara's breasts heaved, the scent of her making him hard. He hadn't imagined he'd ever see her in her hat and boots again. But here she was. And she looked so damn good. His eyes met hers and he could see it, that broken look. It pained him to see it. *Fucking George. She's like a caged, beaten animal now.*

"What are you doing?" Her words switched to defensive as her face flushed.

Jakob smirked. "I was about to ask you the same, Clara."

She puffed out her cheeks, brushing locks of her hair from her shoulder. "Clearing my head."

He raised an eyebrow. "And here I thought you were waiting for a bull rider for some fun."

"Maybe." Clara shrugged. "So, who did you hook up with?"

He frowned. "They asked me to put down the bronco. Vet said he couldn't do anything."

Clara winced. "Sorry, I assumed you… never mind. I've got better things to do than argue with you."

She shook her head and started to walk by him. Lustful wants rattled him. He only took a few long strides to catch her by the arm. She turned with a fiery glare. Her mouth opened to fuss, but he locked lips with her. Gliding his hand across her bare stomach, he slipped under her shirt, groping her breast. She stumbled backward, trapped between him and a stall door.

Her hot fingers worked to claw their way under his wife-beater, riding over his muscled stomach, then travelling to the planes of his back. She moaned as he sucked on her tongue and his free hand started to work her jean skirt up. He placed a knee between her thighs locking her in place. She arched into him, and he pinched her nipple. Another moan and she lashed her tongue out, coaxing his own to enter her mouth.

If she's really up to her old games, then I already know what's waiting under her skirt.

Jakob's hand glided over her bare ass. His smile broke their kiss, and she buried her face in his shoulder. Her hands worked at his belt buckle. His cock throbbed against his jeans; he enjoyed how ravenous he was at her lust. Their heat in their bodies rose with arousal, their desire forgetting all rational thought.

He licked at her ear and goosebumps washed over her skin.

"Dammit, I can't believe I like that," she huffed into him.

At last, his cock was free and in the heat of her soft hands. She stroked him, her thumb firm against the underbelly of his shaft. He moaned as he suckled on her earlobe. Another shiver rattled over her, and he replied with a twist of her nipple. She bit her lip, stifling the urge to shrill in delight. Jakob always loved how she reacted to rough whims.

"Tell me, are you still looking for a bull rider to fuck?" His voice came out, low and husky.

"N-no," she whimpered as he groped her breast tight and rocked his hard dick into her hands. "I found one."

"But you haven't asked me what I want," he teased and kissed her neck.

Circling a thumb on the tip of his cock, she leaned into him, her lips tickling his ear. "You ready to take me for a ride, cowboy?"

His hands abandoned their position. Yanking up on her skirt, he grabbed and lifted her legs up on his hips and slid inside her. She arched, gasping as he ground against her. The stall creaked and shook as he used it to keep her in place. Jakob steadied her with one hand, letting her leg fall as it tippy-toed to meet the height he had risen her to. The other gripped the stall door, clawing into it. He suckled and nibbled at her neck.

I've never felt so hungry for someone before.

She wrapped her arms around his neck, embracing him. A whimper escaped her, and his hunger for her rose. Her nipples hardened under the bikini, and it made his excitement peak. The way her body reacted to his egged him to rock into her faster as her warmth tightened around his cock. She was wet and hot, growing more so with each push and pull. A moan escaped him, his blood rushing. *I haven't messed around in the stalls like this since...* Grunting, he pulled away from her. A sobering coldness hit him.

"Why the hell did you stop?" Clara panted, leaning against the stall gate.

Jakob's mind reeled. "I can't do this again. Not with you."

History is repeating itself. Dammit, she's not looking to be with me.

He started to march away, tucking himself into his pants. Clara caught up to him, straightening her skirt. She called his name, but he refused to look back. He could smell her salty tears and it made his chest ache. Ten years ago, it was all about her. He'd wanted to win her, to beat George Worcestershire, but he had convinced himself it had been false love. When she left, his life stopped. He'd given up bull riding, unable to see the ghost of memories of how many times they had snuck off into these very stables.

Shit, I even sold my truck because her scent still lingered inside it. I'm smitten with her, but I'm just a good time for her and I can't bear to do this all over again. Fucking keep it in your pants, JR.

"Dammit, Jakob!" She ran out in front of him, shoving him with her palms. "Don't fucking do this to me! Not now!"

Their eyes locked and he reflexively charmed her. "Fuck!"

Clara stood there, unable to move, waiting with an eerie calm for his command. He searched his pockets and cursed. The sunglasses had been misplaced, yet again. Looking over at her, he didn't want to leave her in a trance like this. Covering his mouth, his tongue licked the point of a fang and hunger washed over him. He was unsatisfied, both in lust and blood.

A shudder shook his shoulders. *I'm a monster. What does it matter if I push my luck?*

"Clara, do you love me?" he swallowed.

"Yes, but..." her voice trailed off, too exhausted to finish.

"But?" he tensed.

"I fucking hate this small town."

He inhaled, turning away to digest the answer. It was a dick move, charming the truth from her, but he had to know. He *wanted* to know. This whole time she had been so hellbent on leaving Gandersville to the point she took the only opening she thought she had. His stomach knotted, the truth ripping through him.

Maybe she knew I'd just root myself here. Fuck, and now I'm the damn sheriff! Just my damn luck.

"Fucking curse," he muttered, leaning on his knees. "Could I really just let it all go for her?"

"Don't." Clara's arms wrapped around him; she had broken free of the charm sooner than expected. "Don't you dare throw your life away for trash like me."

Anger tore his insides. "Never say that again."

"Jakob, I regret not giving up on George. It was a shit deal from the start, and it only sent me back here, back to you and..."

Her words were lost on him. A wave of drowsiness hit Jakob as the word tilted. The adrenaline in his system had died down, allowing the horse blood to hit him at last. Grabbing Clara by the arm, he had to keep it going, stumbling as he went. Pulling her into an empty stall, he began kissing her again. She responded, working his pants back open. Neither of them had wanted the moment to end as it had.

Pulling away, he untied the knot on her shirt. He pulled her bikini top under her breasts and wrapped his lips around a nipple. She had freed his hard cock and frantically pulled her skirt back up to give him access. He slid back into her heat as her back connected with the back wall. He moaned into her breast, and she pulled at his lower back, urging him to stay close as she rocked against him. Her legs shook and the adrenaline started to kick in, the tranquilizer wavering.

Fuck, it will take me forever to come with this in my system. Good thing Clara's known for her voracious libido.

9

SNARED

Clara's body was on fire. The heat of him added to her flames as they ground against each another. Goosebumps rose on her skin as the tip of Jakob's tongue teased her swollen nipple between his lips. She clung to him like life depended on it. He hadn't released her, after all this time, even when she'd abandoned him in that old pick-up ten years ago.

Her breath caught. *He's so rock hard. How the hell is he teetering on the edge like that?*

She ached from the pleasure of being with him. Long, fast, and hard strokes made her body tremble with ecstasy. A purring rattled from his chest, adding to the erotic moment. He abandoned one nipple and moved to the next. She wriggled against the stall wall, making her shoulder blades ache as she failed to fully arch her back.

Sensing her discomfort, Jakob wrapped his arms around her and pulled her away from the wall.

Jakob shed the wifebeater and abandoned his jeans. Clara followed his lead, wiggling out of her skirt, then tossing her boots and cowgirl hat to the side. After watching her untie the bikini top and letting it fall to the ground, he rushed her like a hungry animal. His hands gripped her waist and lifted her with ease. He placed her on a long, wooden saddle stand and her heart fluttered. The horn nudged her back, making her arch. Pulling her legs over each shoulder, he slid her up on the cantle.

He's been wanting to do this to me for a long time and...

His tongue slid across her like hot silk. She hummed as he ran it across her swollen folds a second time. His fingers gripped her thighs, keeping her legs parted as she took in another stroke of his tongue. Her hands frantically fell behind her, steadying herself on the stand. A gasp escaped her as his tongue slid inside her. Biting her lip, she knew the rule was utter silence, adding to the tension and pleasure.

Dammit, I can't move. I'm going to scream at this rate! We'll be caught!

The saddle made it impossible for her to move. He licked upward and found her clit and began to suckle it. Her thighs ached as his fingers kept her from teetering off or closing around him. Her body shivered. In the past, he had been relentless with the way he played with her body. Tonight, he had at last removed every bit of her dominance. His tongue slid across the front of her pussy, and he began trailing kisses across her hip and ribs.

Her breathing staggered; the sensations boiling through her made her ache to have his cock inside her once more. The stubble of his chin tickled as his lips left a trail between her breasts. As he crested over her collarbone, two fingers entered her, and she tightened in response. His tongue licked across her neck and suckled. Stroking between her thighs, her legs couldn't slow him down. Rough and intoxicating. Teeth grazed her neck, adding to her building orgasm.

"Faster," she panted.

He obeyed, biting her neck harder.

"Rougher," she commanded.

And he did. Fangs broke skin as he twisted his wrist, rubbing her in a sweet spot. She peaked, arching her back. His arm slid under her, the other still stroking hard and fast inside her. Suckling at her neck, he growling as she hummed. Clara's eyes rolled back; her thighs wet with her climax. His fangs lightened their hold, and he licked her neck. She was breathless.

"You taste so amazing," he huffed into the crook of her neck. "Was I too rough?"

"More," she panted. "Don't stop. I want more of you."

Her hand found his chest and slid downward. His cock was still rock-hard, and she began stroking him. Meeting his gaze, his eyes were that of a reptile, yellow with slits for pupils. It added to her lust. Something red painted his bottom lip as he weighed her words.

He's a monster and I want him to keep fucking me.

"Clara, I don't know if I can come," he confessed, turning her on the saddle so her feet touched the ground. "Look, I need you to know..."

She melted, kneeling so she could lick his throbbing erection. He lost his words, leaning on the saddle stand as she took him inside her mouth. Her lips ached with the girth of his dick. Rubbing her tongue on the soft shaft, she deep throated him, over and over again. Each time the tip of his dick rode down the back of her throat, he'd throb and moan. She sucked long and hard until her cheeks ached with effort.

Breathless, she took a moment of leave, stroking him with both hands. Looking up, she locked eyes with him. He panted, the fangs in his mouth only adding to her desire to have him eat her alive. She ran her tongue up and down his shaft, suckling on occasion to add to his agony. Sweat glistened on their bodies, the night air cooling and his breath steaming from his lips like a draconic beast.

"Fuck me," she begged. "Fucking come on me or in my ass, but fuck me with this, please."

Again, she ran her tongue against his length. She started suckling on the tip of his penis, her lips sliding to the edge of the cap and back again. Huffing, he looked pained for a moment. Another large puff of steam left him, his yellow eyes bright with hunger.

"Stand up and bend over the saddle."

He shuddered in anticipation as her hands slid up his thighs. She wanted to feel all of him under her hands, riding over his hips, waving over his torso, before cupping his jaw. A deep kiss lingered between them, but his hands stayed firm on the saddle stand. She sucked on his bottom lip, the iron on his tongue strange and alluring. He watched her with hungry eyes, then she bent over.

Clara spread her stance, bending provocatively until her breasts pressed against the saddle. At last, his hands abandoned the stand. Starting at the base of her neck, one hand trailed down her spine like hot wax. The heat of his hand spilled over her ass and fingers dove back inside her. She moaned, leaning into his stroking. He retrieved them, the tip of his dick pressing against her swollen lips. He slid inside, slow and deep.

Christ, his dick is so damn big and hard.

She wiggled, giving him just enough room to glide all the way in, his hips tight against hers. He pulled slow and steady, teasing her as he nearly pulled out, only to dive back in with the same agonizing speed. She squeezed around his cock, wanting him to stay inside her, wanting to ride him and please herself until she couldn't contain the feeling anymore. His hands gripped her hips, continuing to rock, in and out, faster and faster.

She let out a tiny gasp as his balls slapped against her clit, still tender from his sucking.

Jakob towered over her, grinding her with relentless drive. The saddle stand threatened to topple over with each connection. Clara's resolve wavered as yelps escaped her with each erogenous rush. He pushed hard against her, his body laying heavy on top of her now. His tongue slid over her shoulder, and he nuzzled her ear.

"Will you finally give me permission to go all the way this time?"

Exasperated, she tried to glance back at him. He bit her shoulder then licked the spot. This was a side of him she had almost seen in the past, a predator enjoying his meal, slow and ravenous all in a single stride. The tip of his cock pushed against her back door. She leaned into him, forcing the tip to enter further.

"Last time I tried this, you nearly clawed my eyes out," he laughed, daring to press further inside.

"I missed out on something incredible." She pushed against him, forcing him to slide in deeper. "I'm tired of us pulling away before either of us are through. Fuck me like you've always wanted, like I've been needing you to fuck me since that night."

He pressed hard into her, and she yelped, "You're not asking a cowboy to ride you anymore. You're wanting the bull to mount you, own you, make you mine."

She arched her back, rocking against his aching loins, *daring* him by saying, "Then show me the difference."

His hips rocked. "I won't be gentle, Clara."

"Good, I'm tired of being treated like a porcelain doll," her voice shrilled.

"I won't stop, even if you beg me." His hands were like fiery snakes riding over her hips and up the sides of her torso. "You're going to meet your match."

"Fucking prove it."

She tried to stand, but a hand rushed to the back of her neck, pushing her firmly against the saddle.

"Didn't you hear me?" Jakob's voice came out in a low, animalistic rumble. "You're mine. You want me to let loose, to fuck you how I've wanted since the day we first came back here, in this very stall? Your scent haunted me when you left. Wrecked me, like I'm going to wreck you. I want you to claw at my flesh, cry my name in pleasure, and beg for me to let you go only to come crawling back for more."

"I want that! I want all of that and so much more."

Holy hell, I shook him and I'm about to get the fucking of my life.

10

RIDING THE BULL

Jakob could feel himself slipping deeper into his Chupacabra instincts. The scent of her was haunting and delightful, like a slice of peach rolling across his tongue. The taste of it sweet and savory on the air only added to his wants. He didn't want to drink blood; he simply wanted to mate with her until he exhausted himself. The horse tranquilizers were easing off, Clara's blood invigorating and freeing him from it. He'd never tasted human blood before tonight, but he only wanted hers for the rest of his life. He throbbed in her warmth, a low growl rolling through him, and she tightened.

Jakob tightened his grip on her neck. "You've ruined me," he said as she shuddered with delight.

"Don't stop." She rocked her body against him. "F-faster."

A growl drummed through him, scales surfacing in blue and silvery patches. "Beg me."

"Fuck me faster," she panted, her legs trembling.

"Say my name," his voice hissed in her ear. "Prove that it's me that you want."

The rhythm of his rocking hips against her made her tighten with each push. She couldn't stop the orgasms rising with each motion, keeping her from finding her voice as she gasped. Hearing the choked attempts to scream his name delighted him. Her body was hot, slick under his torso. His free hand slid back across her hip, forcing its way between her wet thighs. She shrieked as his fingers rubbed her pussy, circling her clit with sodden fingertips.

I want to cum, but I want her to beg for it first.

"You done yet?" He pushed hard and deep into her, his fingers sliding inside her. "You know what I want. Say my name."

"J-Ja." Breathless, she still defied him as she rocked her hips. "Jakob! Don't you dare stop."

Impatience rattled him. He released her neck, swooping an arm under her and forcing her to stand as he continued thrusting from behind. Her legs shook, and he denied her the support of the saddle or its stand. His fingers stroked in and out of her, his arm hugging her against him as he groped her breast with the other. Clara squirmed, reaching out for the saddle, only to have him pull her back. Walking backward until the stall door rattled against his back, Jakob stayed where she couldn't reach anything else. He leaned back on the door, tilting her into his own, cuddling her.

"Beg me to finish," he growled.

"N-No."

Nuzzling at her neck, he found the wound where he'd bitten her. Hungry, he licked at it, willing it to bleed once more. With Jakob suckling her neck, goosebumps rolled across her skin like a breeze on a lake's surface. She moaned again, tightening on his fingers.

"I want on top," she fussed. "Let me on top, please."

He ignored her as her hands cupped his own where he stroked her pussy and pushed into her ass. "Beg me to finish."

"Jakob, fucking let me on top." It was her turn to growl. "Jakob, please!"

He released her. She spun. Pushing down on his shoulders, she didn't seem phased by the slitted, yellow eyes, fangs under his lips, or the patches of scales. Her want for him was as feral as his own and he groaned. Sliding to the ground, the stall door banged with their movements. She straddled him.

Biting her lip, she let him slide back into the warm tightness of her backdoor. Locking eyes, he throbbed inside her and she began rocking on his hard cock. Bracing herself with one hand on his shoulder, the other dove between them and she played with herself. She moaned, staring into his eyes with a hunger he had thought only he was capable of feeling. Gripping her hips, he rocked with her, allowing them to push and pull with deeper strides.

"Do you love me?" She narrowed her eyes. "Tell me Jakob."

The question made him throb, nearing his peak. "I fucking love you. Always have."

"Fucking come for me, Jakob." Her body stiffened, an orgasm building in her body. "Please, come for me. I want you to come for me, Jakob!"

Wrapping his arms around her, his lips wrapped around a nipple, sucking long and hard, he ground in and out, fast and hard. A moan erupted from deep at his core and he peaked, hard and stiff inside her. Another moan and he released her breast and tilted his head back. He reached his climax, and she clawed into his shoulders and rocked on him, keeping his orgasm riding out longer than he'd ever know was possible.

When he couldn't take it anymore, he pulled her back to him, kissing her deeply. She stilled, the tension in their bodies fading as they released numbing pleasure from their bodies. She cuddled into him, shivering as the cold air around them crept over, their fires dying. She nuzzled his chest, both of them left breathless and panting.

"Christ, I didn't think you'd ever come," she laughed into him, and he scoffed.

"I almost thought you'd fuck me into eternity."

Her face heated against his chest. "Thank you."

Inhaling deeply, he leaned his head against hers and asked, "For what?"

"For loving me, despite it all."

"I could say the same."

Pulling away, she cupped his jaw and searched his eyes. "What are you?"

Scales had started to recede, but he couldn't deny this. Not anymore. "You wouldn't believe me if I told you."

"I don't fucking care." She kissed his lips, hard. "All I know is that you know how to fuck a girl and fuck her right."

Jakob laughed. "Sometimes I wonder which of us is the bigger monster in this small town."

Without warning, she stood and started picking up her clothes. He stared at her, confused. Clara wiggled into her skirt, circled once, found her bikini top, and tossed him his pants. Jakob's heart skipped a beat, the past drowning him with what would come next. Stumbling to his feet, he started to pull his legs into his pants, watching her.

"Why rush to leave?" He couldn't hide the panic in his voice.

She put her cowgirl hat on. "I can't let them find me here with you," she said, picking straw from her hair.

"Why not?" He glared at her, lost in his anger.

"Are you fucking kidding me?" She slipped on a boot and tossed him his wifebeater. "If this small town learned the town whore fucked the sheriff, both of us will have hell to pay."

"Clara, I won't keep this a secret."

Slamming on her other boot, she was on her feet, across the stall with a nail poking into his chest. "I left this shit ten years ago. If you let it slip, it'll make the front-page news. And..."

"And what?" His chest heaved as he bowed over her. "So what if the town knows?"

Her face reddened. "You don't get it."

She shoved past him, her voice cracking.

There it is. She can't hide and she hates herself. Seeing and hearing it from the gossipers eats her alive. "Do you even care about how I feel?"

She stopped at the stable door, refusing to turn and look at him.

"You better not leave town this time."

Shoving the door open, she murmured, "My wings are already clipped."

Jakob's heart pounded with anxiety. After all of that, the confessions of love and seeing a glimpse of his true nature, she still chose to run. He leaned against the saddle stand, lost. She had done this that faithful night of her bachelorette party. Every time he made any ground with her, she ran. He didn't understand it, the fear of loving someone for real. Her love for George Worcestershire was like a royal wedding, but their affair had been kept secret.

What happened? Did I do or say something to make you act this way?

A hushed whisper and crackle of his radio brought him back to who he was, who she hated: the small-town sheriff.

"You there, Sheriff Regadera?" Suzie's voice sputtered across the silence.

Reluctant, he walked over and answered, "Yeah. What is it?"

"We need someone to come fill in the nightshift," Suzie demanded.

"What happened to old Bill?" He leaned on the table, shooting a dirty glare at his uniform shirt. "It's his turn; I'm at the rodeo."

"I told him that, but he's got crutches, Jakob," she whined. "It's Friday night and you know that someone's going to have to go sort things out at 8 Seconds."

He hung his head in defeat. "Give me time to shower. I'm a mess, Mrs. Suzie."

"Just make it out there before the first fight breaks out."

He dropped the radio and began pacing the stall like a caged tiger. Flashes of the last several minutes still rolled through his body. Swallowing, he looked back to the tack table. He had left everything there before his ride. It was bad enough he had bittersweet memories of Clara in this small space, but her scent was everywhere, on *him.* Anger coursed through him, and he kicked the saddle stand across the stall. Every fiber in his body seethed with hurt and self-hatred.

Fuck. I'm back to where I started ten years ago. I don't know who I hate more: Clara or myself.

11

8 SECONDS

Clara sat silently in the passenger seat. Brandye glared over. All attempts to weasel an answer had failed. She made it clear it was time to go and go now. Without further prying, they'd loaded up and left, the rodeo lit brightly in the darkness of the countryside and the roar of locals cheering on the riders.

Clara spotted another stray piece of hay in her hair and pulled it out.

"Are we going to talk about what the hell happened to you?" Brandye lifted an eyebrow, twisting her lips. "Bite marks, hay... really, Clara?"

"Nope." Clara shot her a cautionary look. "I got what I came for and now I want to go home."

"Oh no we don't." Brandye turned, placing distance between Clara and her rundown shit-shack.

"Brandye-wine," she huffed. "Take me home. Please."

"Don't tell me you don't need a drink." Her eyebrows raised high.

Clara forced a smirk. "Yeah. I need a few drinks."

Leaning back into the seat, she stared up at the roof. Her body was still hot and buzzing as the phantom touch of Jakob's hands on her body made her shudder. She would have continued if they hadn't exhausted themselves. Closing her eyes tight, she shoved him from her mind. Echoes of the past sent a tidal wave of regret, the weight of it smashing down on her. Years ago, she had convinced herself she'd be settling for Jakob, but instead, she had settled with...

"Shit." She leaned forward, pained by the realization. "Have you ever looked back and wondered why the hell you thought something was a good idea?"

"Oh yeah." Brandye pulled into the parking lot, the truck squeaking to a stop. "And I just make an excuse. Then it's time for a glass of wine or an old fashioned to remind me I will do better next time."

"What if you fucked over your next time?" Clara climbed out and followed Brandye to the line at the door of the club. "Like royally fucked up the only second chance you had?"

Brandye narrowed her eyes, weighing each word. "You better hope you're just meant to cross paths and be together then."

"ID's?" The bouncer maintained a neutral expression as he scanned their licenses into the machine. "Hands."

They held up their fists, a blue stamp saying, *8 Seconds Bar & Dance Hall,* were smudged across them. Inside, the smell of stale cigarette smoke still lingered in the building, despite changing over to non-smoking ages ago. Neon signs from ales and beers glowed above the bartender stations throughout the dark warehouse. In the back, line dancers were mid-swing in a cult classic, *Boot Scootin' Boogie,* as Brandye dragged her through the crowd.

Leaning on the bar, she managed to grab a seat and wait for her drink. She didn't care what Brandye ordered; she just wanted to get hammered. A flash of Jakob's fingers gripping her hips crossed her mind, and she turned to the bartender to escape it. He slid an old fashioned to her, and she started chugging. All she wanted was to drown, to forget she'd let her guard down, that *he'd* let his guard down. Nothing in her life had felt more real than those moments in the stall, and she had abandoned it.

I'm a monster. He loves me and I can't accept it. What the fuck is wrong with me?

Brandye turned to face her and blinked. The glass emptied and clunking on the bar top, she tilted her head at Clara. Ignoring her friend's cautionary glare, she waved the bartender back. An old fashioned wasn't strong enough to forget the lustful vibrations still shaking her core.

"Two Sambucas," Clara announced. *Need to get shitfaced. I don't want to remember our time together. It'll only keep hurting.*

"That's some hard shit. You don't have to get me a shot." Brandye sipped on her own old fashioned.

"They're both for me." *Faster, stronger, drunker, longer... Ha! Daft Punk has nothing on me!*

"What the hell happened?" Brandye choked on her drink, adding, "And who the hell did you hook up with?"

Clara took the first Sambuca in a single gulp. *Jakob. I can't resist him, I want him, he's... no fuck this. I need to get over him just like I got over Asshole fucking my so-called friend Sharon. Fuck you, Sharon.*

"Don't tell me." Putting her drink down, Brandye leaned in and whispered, "Did you go back there and fuck Jakob? Are you kidding me?"

Clara gave her a side glance, but the arriving second shot came and was gone. *If she weren't my real friend, I'd throw my drink across the bar. Jakob, of course with Jakob. You know I loved him. You caught us that night at my bachelorette party and never said a damn thing. You even asked if I wanted out of the wedding. You knew. And you were right. I fucking love him.*

"Clara!" Brandye rubbed her temples. "Are you out of your mind? If the town gets wind, fuck, if Geor..."

"Don't you dare mention that asshole's name." She spun, leaning back on the bar top, her body still warm from the alcohol. "I just need to find someone else to ride. After that, I'll be fine. Fuck Jakob. Fuck this town. Fuck... Trevor?"

Her eyes caught a familiar face. A grin crept across her face. She had her target. Standing, she wobbled as if hit by a rogue wave. Straightening, she took a minute to adjust her girls and fluff her hair. Hay flakes fell and she marched off, ready to take down her prey. He was chatting it up with some fellow fraternity boys as she closed the gap. She slid a hand up his bicep and shoulder, and he spun and paled.

"Miss Williams?" His momentary panic didn't faze her.

"Call me, Clara," she cooed, batting her eyes up at him. "Didn't think I'd run into you here of all places, Trevor."

He swallowed, releasing a nervous laugh. "Yeah, actually, I'm here with some friends."

She glanced at the other boys and winked. "Hi, friends."

"Look, Clara? I'm actually here with..."

Her scalp lit on fire as she stumbled backward, her hat falling to the floor as she was dragged. "What the fuck!"

"No bitch touches my man like that," she heard a female screech.

Gritting her teeth, she managed to spin herself into a more controlling pose, her hair obscuring her view. Seeing the cheap Wal-Mart flip flops as the cool outside air hit her skin, Clara unraveled. Reaching out, she grabbed a fistful of shirt and yanked the girl forward. Her grip faltered on Clara's hair, and she stood tall, drunk and fuming. Like the crack of a whip, Clara's palm connected with a makeup caked cheek. The College brat wide-eyed, ears ringing.

"Don't fucking touch me." Clara stood, unshaking.

The girl cupped her face, snarling as her hair loosened from its bun. "You bitch!"

She came at Clara, and her other hand snapped against the other cheek. "Try me."

Tears welled up and Clara smirked. The girl had challenged Gandersville's most notorious cat-fight champion. Nails were next and if the cops took too long, clothes would be ripped, and hair pulled out. The college girl recovered and tackled Clara, knocking the wind from her. But Clara didn't back down. Her claws were out, already scraping across the girl's back.

She retreated, flicking Clara the bird.

Clara hissed, a warning for her to back down.

Hands on hips, she stood proud in her drunken haze. Blue and red lights illuminated the back of the building like a disco ball. The siren had been silenced, announcing their arrival. She turned, too damn tried to run like the college girl. Chin high she watched as the truck came to a stop.

"Clara." Jakob's voice came the megaphone, bringing her a wave of nausea. "What did I say about starting trouble?"

He stepped out of the driver's side, his uniform in disarray. He hadn't bothered to button it. His mouth held a deep scowl, his eyes hidden under his sunglasses. She wasn't sure what he was waiting for. And she was too fucking drunk to run away. *Fuck it.*

Throwing out her arms, she inhaled deeply. "Come on. Arrest me." She raised her chin, too prideful to back down. "I'll let you cage me this time. You're welcome."

Snorting, he marched across the span and pulled her arms behind her. She closed her eyes; the cold steel handcuffs a harsh contrast to the heat of his hands. Biting her lip, she waited for the questions or fight she had put into motion, but it never came. She had abandoned him in the stalls, running from the idea of having a meaningful relationship.

"How much did you drink?" His voice dropped to a muttered rumble.

"Not enough."

Shaking his head, he helped her into the passenger side. "I'm taking you back to the station."

"I know." She refused to look at his face.

Getting into the driver's side, he flipped the lights off. "Is it so terrible to think we could..."

Jakob's words failed, and he ignored her the whole way back. Clara hated herself, hated that even now, neither of them could deny their mutual attraction.

Am I cursed? Are we both cursed?

12

Jailhouse

Clara's silence only added to Jakob's agony. There were many things he wanted to ask, but he knew she would never tell him. Glancing over, he saw that she had dozed off. Her head was cocked back and snoring. Sighing, he reached over and coaxed her until her head was in his lap. At least, she would be more comfortable. She nuzzled against his thigh, the smell of Sambuca and whiskey rising to his nostrils. He reached down to pull her hair from her face but stopped.

Last time I saw her this smashed, she'd been celebrating her bachelorette party.

"You didn't want to go, did you?" he muttered, heaving another sigh.

They had arrived at the station to find the building and parking lot completely empty. Pulling into the reserved spot by the door, he shut the truck off. He leaned on his steering wheel and looked back down to her. Her eyes were open, the blue visible in the dim glowing streetlamps. She searched his face, and he twisted his lips, waiting to see what venom she'd spew. *Here it comes. That folding of the brow, the parting of frowning lips.*

"How the hell can you see anything at night?" She rolled up, yawning, and stretching.

"Wait, what?" He stared at her back, licking his lips as he imagined her bent over a saddle. The idea sent a shiver through him. "I got us here wearing them, didn't I? What does it matter?"

Jakob steeled himself, ignoring the sudden rise of lust. He walked around and helped her out. She didn't say anything, stumbling as he guided her through the station. Pausing at the desk, he checked her skirt pockets. She laughed and muttered a slurred something under her breath, too difficult to decipher. Emptying the keys and her cellphone onto the desk, he led her into the containment cell. He let her sit before closing the sliding barred door. Sitting at his desk, he began writing his report.

Bing! He paused and glanced at her phone but returned to writing. A quick glance at the screen showed the text that popped up.

[BrandyeWine: Call me if you need a ride from the jailhouse again. Love you!]

None of my business.

He cleared his throat and tossed his sunglasses aside. Again, he started reviewing the reports and cursed old Billy for his shit writing and Suzie for overexplaining. Powering through, he took solace in the fact that he managed a small town and not a big city. A shiver rattled his shoulders. The report of the horse had been reported over the radio, and Suzie had jotted down the details. Jakob's eyes danced across the paper, reading the cursive as he covered his mouth. Glancing over, he saw that Clara had laid down on the bench and he hoped she'd fallen back to sleep.

A feral dog tore into the Hawthorne's bronco. She was in her stall for a broken leg. Poor Barret almost got rolled on by the horse when it happened. Anyhow, they called Doc Samson, but he had left...

Bing! Jakob skipped a line at the sound.

...he had left because Little Jenny's dog was having puppies. They got the X-rays and there's no saving a horse with a break in that many pieces, shattered like a broken vase. Well, we were trying to reach Jakob when...

Bing! Stopping, he looked over at Clara's phone, the texts still visible in preview mode.

[Tommy: Hey Sexy]

[Tommy: You ready for some fun tonight?]

He snorted, ignoring it, and continued to read.

...a hold of Jakob when crazy old Mr. Baker said the Chupacabra got to it first. There's no such thing; the boys think a coyote came in there and spooked before anyone found out.

"Well, Mr. Baker isn't as crazy as you think, Suzie." Jakob signed the paper and slid it away.

Bing!

[Tommy: Tell me what you're wearing? I'm betting it's those lacy black panties I love so much.]

Jokes on you buddy. She ain't got anything on under her skirt tonight.

Jakob twisted his lips, glaring at the screen. Drumming his fingers, he looked at Clara, then returned to her phone.

Who the fuck is Tommy?

Bing!

[Tommy: How about this: I'll show you mine if you show me yours?]

Narrowing his eyes, he grabbed the cell phone. He slid his finger across the screen, unlocking it, prompting a passcode. Raising an eyebrow, he smirked. Without fail, it was her birthday, and it took him promptly to the texts between Clara and Tommy. He began scrolling up, the sexting marathon unveiled. Heat flushed his face, sexy teaser pics and racy words sending him into a wave of lust and jealousy.

Inhaling deeply, he glanced over his shoulder, making sure she hadn't caught him. His thumbs flew over the keys as he typed.

[Clara: Not tonight. I'm busy.]

[Tommy: Busy? Don't make me beg ;)]

Jakob scoffed.

[Clara: I have better things to do.]

[Tommy: Better and bigger than this <DICK PIC>]

Jakob's jealousy flared. Rage consumed him, ceasing all rational thought. He unbuckled his belt and unzipped his pants, freeing his hardened length, which throbbed from Clara's provocative photos.

Click!

[Clara: Definitely bigger and better <DICK PIC WITH MIDDLE FINGER>]

"What the hell are you doing with my phone?" Clara's voice startled him, and he dropped her phone to the floor. "Jakob, give it back."

"Look, Clara, it kept ringing and..." He spun, standing.

"Were you fucking taking dick pics on my phone?" She blinked, glaring at his raging hard on, a smile filing her face. Shrugging, she laughed. "Granted, I wouldn't mind adding yours to the collection."

Spinning around, he tucked himself away. Grabbing the phone off the floor, he turned it off and tossed it on the desk. Jakob leaned against the tabletop, his emotions raging in his self-hatred. He waited for her to rail him further, crack the small-town sheriff jab or something else to remind him she couldn't accept him. Nothing. He looked over his shoulder, watching her as she turned away and marched back. Her boot slipped, her body still drunk and slow, and her head connected with the corner of the bench.

Jakob opened the cell door and flew to her side. She sat up, hissing as a rivulet of blood slid down her forehead. Something inside him shifted. He pulled her head to him and ran his tongue across the sweet aromatic liquid. The blood hot and thick on his tongue, he kissed the swollen knot forming, sucking on the wound for a moment. She sat still, calm even. Alcohol tinged in the flavor, riding down his throat as he swallowed, and Jakob jerked back.

"Clara..."

"Your eyes." She glared at him in awe. "Those golden eyes. I love them." He stood, reaching for his sunglasses, but she grabbed his arm, stopping him. "Don't leave."

He closed his eyes, feeling hopeless. "Clara, I can't risk charming you."

She laughed, gripping his shirt to steady herself. "You charmed me a long time ago. I have a feeling it doesn't last ten years."

He smirked. "I'm not that good."

"Stay here." Her hands relaxed, sliding to his jeans and unzipped them.

"Don't," he whispered, grabbing her hands, afraid to open his eyes. "We can't. Not here."

"You can't waste a hard-on like that." She pouted, shoving his hands off, letting her hot fingers wrap around his shaft. "Let me have some fun first."

"You're drunk." His heart raced, his resolve crumbling with each beat.

"And you just took a dick pic on my phone." She circled her tongue on the tip. "And that deserves a punishment."

"Well, I don't think Tommy liked that idea quite like you." He breathed, the wave of arousal drowning him. A flash of the picture with her fingers in her pussy made him moan. "Clara, stop. We can't do this."

She paused. "Open your eyes and make me stop."

He opened one golden eye and looked down at her. Licking his lips, he shut it and exhaled, long and slow. Nothing about this had anything but raw want driving it into the next ridiculous moment. Reaching one hand out, he found a bar to balance on. His shoulders relaxed in defeat. He wanted this as much as she did, and the idea that she'd rather suck on his cock than sext with Tommy gave Jakob satisfaction.

"That's what I thought."

Her wet, silken tongue connected with the top of his hard cock. Sliding him between her lips, she leaned into him and let his dick ride until he hit the back of her throat. She wiggled her head, letting him go a little deeper, tighter. As slowly as she'd taken his length in, she pulled out with the pop of her lips. Again, her tongue circled the head and repeated the agonizing deep dive into the wet heat of her mouth.

Jakob leaned into her, wanting to linger longer. The suckling made him moan as another pop of lips left him cold. Clara started trailing kisses from the tip to the base of his shaft. Fingertips kept his throbbing erection firm against her lips. Hints of her tongue and the occasional sucking of the tender underbelly made him weak in the knees. Something about the way she made love to his cock made him hungry to fuck her, just to end the teasing banter.

Her hands gripped his ass cheeks. Once more, he slid between her tight lips, to the silken road to the back of her throat. Another moan escaped him, and she began pushing and pulling. Shifting his stance, she followed. He braced himself against the bars of the containment cell.

His eyes cracked open, staring down at her as they locked stares. The pop of her lips on the tip of his dick made him grunt and shudder, again.

"Was wondering when you'd join the party," she smirked, running her tongue along his shaft. "I want to see your face when you come, Jakob."

He ran his tongue over his fangs and teeth. "Careful, or you'll make me nibble you again."

"Is that a promise?" she smirked.

Hell, yes.

13

Time to Go

Clara loved that look in his eyes, a mixture of admiration and desire, simple and raw. Jakob wanted *her*. And only *her*. That heavy-lidded glare said it all, and more, and it made her wet, knowing what he would do to her body. She made love to his throbbing cock, kissing the soft flesh deeply, passionately. Her mind wandered, questioning her own agenda and the events of the last few weeks.

I can handle settling down in this town as long as I have him.

Daring the golden eyes to watch her, she took him back into her mouth. Her cheeks ached with the effort, his moaning driving her to release one ass cheek and dive her hand between her thighs. The blow job had made her wet, throbbing to have him enter her once more. Her fingers inside her pussy, she moaned on his cock, and it throbbed in response. At last, his greed surfaced.

Thick fingers tangled and gripped the hair on her head. He thrust in and out of her mouth, the effort making her break from their stare. Her other hand fell away from him, joining the other under her skirt. Jakob was on the verge of coming, his dick hard as a rock as he rode across her tongue. Another moan as she circled her clit, her body still sensitive from earlier in the day. His grip tightened. The tip diving deep into the back of her throat. Both of them moaned as they peaked, her thighs wet as she swallowed the hot liquid.

Jakob pulled out slowly, a string of her saliva lingering between her lips and the tip of his dick. They locked eyes. Each of them panting still flushed from their orgasms.

BUZZ!

"Fuck!" Jakob squatted, shielding himself behind Clara, keeping his distance from the front door.

"W-what the hell is that sound?" Clara wiped her lips.

"Someone's coming through the front door." Jakob patted his shirt pockets. "Shit. Where did they go?"

Clara watched his rising panic, and without thinking, she cupped his jaw and kissed him. Her tongue dipped between his lips, rubbing against a fang before pulling away. She searched his face, the blue-grey scales were gone, and his eyes had returned to brown. He blinked at her, and it excited her knowing she could bring out and put away the beast of the Chupacabra with such ease.

"There," she whispered. "Your eyes are brown, and the scales have disappeared."

"T-thank you." He brushed her hair from her forehead, a bruise already forming. "You need to be home. That's gonna hurt in the morning."

"Oh, Jakob!" Suzie screeched. "Is that Clara Wor-Williams?"

"Hey, Suzie," Clara drawled.

Jakob stood, calm and reserved. "She slipped and hit her head."

Clara smirked; glad Suzie couldn't see her face. *Slipped on his dick and gave him head. Ha!*

"Oh dear." She entered the cell, erasing Clara's smirk. "Are you alright?"

"I'll live. I wouldn't be here if I hadn't started trouble at the bar. It's my fault really."

"Aren't you too old to be up to your old habits, young lady?" Suzie seemed as if time hadn't passed. The silver-haired woman in cat eyeglasses put her hands on her hip. "Jakob, you take her home. I'll lock up."

"Why are you here?" Jakob looked at the clock on the far wall. "And at almost three in the morning?"

"I forgot my pocketbook and just couldn't sleep thinking about it." She spun on her heel and grabbed a purse out of the front desk's largest drawer. "I advise you just to take the poor thing home. She's had it rough."

Clara blinked, stunned to hear her Ex's number one fan's pity.

"I just got wind what really happened in the city between you two." She sighed, her brow furrowing. "A real damn shame, but I hope you find someone worth keeping. Maybe Jakob might be a good option."

Clara's face heated. "Thank ... you?"

"Mrs. Suzie that's rather..." Jakob's face turned red and his eyes shot off to the side as if caught doing something. "You shouldn't assume..."

"Oh, come on, Jakob." She cackled, hands still on her hips. "You two have been giving each other puppy dog eyes since high school. I'm shocked I didn't catch you bending her over your desk just now."

Another wave of heat hit Clara's face. *Has it always been that obvious to the whole town? Why hadn't anyone said anything sooner? Why not pry and twist things like they always do with every aspect of my life? Had she missed something? Exactly how long has the damn town known about me and Jakob fucking on the side?*

Panic filled her face.

"Don't you look so shocked," Suzie laughed again. "Even a small town has its secrets, darlin' and we all secretly knew about you two. Damn shame you didn't end up together. Pride is a terrible thing, but at least you're home where you belong."

Do I belong here? She looked at Jakob's pursed lips, his eyes flickering a hint of gold. She jumped to her feet. *What on earth has him shifting again?*

"Thank you, Suzie." Clara sidled to block Jakob from Suzie's prying eyes. "I didn't think... why didn't anyone say something?"

"About what?" Suzie pulled out her keys from her coat pocket. "You two sneaking off together?"

"Yeah." Clara knew if she turned the questions on the old woman, she'd rush off. "Normally shit around here is front page news."

"Honey, you've got much to learn." She shuffled for the exit, her back to them now. "No one comes between love and lust. People kill for money, for power ... and love. You don't mess with that hornets' nest."

With that, she disappeared, and Clara spun to face Jakob. His face was pale and gaunt. His eyes shifted to gold and he searched the air. Lips tight, he had that panic building in his face once more.

"It doesn't matter if they know," Clara shrugged, leaning against the bars.

"I don't care that they know about us, but..." He inhaled deep, steadying his nerves. "I can't shake the feeling they just might know about this." He motioned to his eyes. Clara bit her lip. "And why the hell has no one confronted me about it? They have to know, right?"

"Shit." *This whole time I didn't realize he had far more at risk staying here than I will ever fathom.* "Take me home," Clara said, redirecting the conversation. "We can talk on the way there."

He grabbed her hand and led her out of the cell, gathering their things at his desk. His jaw was set tight, eyes still glazed with the wave of thoughts drowning him. She followed, silent and measuring his every expression and movement. Suzie winked at them as he led her out, again a tight hand gripping hers. She was the only thing keeping him from losing it. Like always, he helped her into the passenger side, walked around, and sat. He froze.

"Can you drive?" Clara realized the weight of his situation crashing down on him.

He looked at her at last, his voice a mumble. "Did you hear how my mother died?"

Clara bit her lip, remembering the rumors. "She was shot ... for trespassing."

His eyes shifted to gold. "Yeah, but what I thought no one knew..."

"What really happened? Wasn't she a maid for the Worcestershire Estate?" Clara's chest swelled, the dots connecting, and she shared his building anxiety. "That fight between you and George in high school... don't..." A wave of nausea hit her. She leaned forward and covered her mouth. The untapped anger, the hurt in his face that she would be engaged and marrying. Tears welled up.

"He shot her. Caught her eating one of the old cows." He covered his face and took in an unsteady breath. "He fucking shot her. And left her out there. Not once apologized, not once gave a flying fuck. His dad saw it all, and they dragged me to the barn to *beat the beast out of me.*"

Another wave of emotions rolled through her, rattling her to her core. "The limp. Your limp is from..."

"You weren't the only one aiming to leave town, Clara." At last, he wrangled in his panic, starting the truck, and leaving the station far behind. "It was either the football scholarship or hoping I could join the PBR and compete regionally in bull riding. George knew that. I had confided in him. I though he was my friend."

Clara frowned, looking out the window, unable to face Jakob as she took it all in. *Yeah, he's really good at taking your dreams and choking you with them.*

"He broke the fucking bat over my shin." Anger rose in his voice. "And when he cornered me at the rodeo and rubbed it in my face, you were planning to elope and celebrating your bachelorette party…"

Clara's eyes widened, that night coming back. "You didn't do your last ride. That's why you were there before the rest." She turned to him, but he wouldn't meet her eyes as they turned down the last road toward the Worcestershire estate. "You didn't quit bull riding. You got suspended. And with your leg, football got fucked."

He pulled the truck to the door, shutting off the engine to look at her. "Sorry. I can't be the one to sweep you off your feet and take you away from here."

Clara glared around the property, thinking back to their youth, to the days she'd catch him shirtless, repairing the barn or sneaking off to fuck in the tool shed. Memories of his mother were blurry, fleeting. She didn't speak much English, but she had been kind, spoiling guests with homemade sweets and cold iced tea.

"Do you hate this place?"

"No," he whispered. "A lot of pride went into this heap. Mom loved it. And now someone I care about lives here."

She turned to him. He cupped her jaw and kissed her deeply and passionately. They pulled away, slow, still gazing at one another but with a new sense of self.

"I made a horrible mistake," Clara muttered.

"You wanted out."

"You were hurting, and I was too narcissistic to..." His lips pressed against hers, silencing her.

"You mind if I crash here? I've got an issue to take care of, to get out of my system."

He was getting out of the truck, and she scrambled to meet him by the headlights, resting her hands on his chest. "Where are you going?"

"It's a new moon." He shuddered, then his eyes began to glow. "It's the one night I can't control my shifting or running through the pastures."

She kissed him and his eyes calmed. "Stay with me, just a little longer. Until I fall asleep."

14.

The Couch

J akob couldn't say no to her, to that face. She pushed on his chest, and he allowed her to spin him around and prod him up the porch steps and through the door. The living room was bare besides the few boxes in a corner and a leather Victorian loveseat in the center of the room. Clara shut the door and slid the lock in place. He spun to face her, an eyebrow lifting high. She began to shed her clothes and he tilted his head.

"Clara, are you still drunk?"

Wiggling out of the skirt and pulling off her boots, she scoffed. "We both know I'm not belligerent and my buzz died the moment you arrested me."

"I'm serious. It's a new moon and control is..." She stalked across the space. "Clara, this is a bad idea. Even my parents limited..."

She shushed him, tugging off his uniform shirt and pulled up on his wifebeater. "You have to get naked to change, right, Mr. Chupacabra?"

He laughed, looking away in disbelief. "Yeah, but not like this. I don't usually need assistance from a hot, naked chick to make that part happen."

"Well tonight you do." She tugged on his wifebeater again and he caved, taking it off. "There, now let me help with this too."

Her skillful fingers worked until his pants fell away.

His face heated, agonizing over the new moon and his need to feed had hit a new level, including his sex drive. As a child, his father would get a hotel room for three days during the new moon. He always shrugged and frowned at Jakob, saying, *that's a dangerous night for me. Your mother could kill a man with stamina like that.*

"Aren't you exhausted?" Her hands were hot across his torso as she shoved him backward. "You've had quite the day. I mean, you and I, we've been at each other twice and..."

Another hard push and the back of his knees hit the loveseat. He sat. With his golden eyes, he didn't need lights to see her in the dark, to see her pink erect nipples and the goosebumps rippling across her body in a flurry of excitement. He throbbed, his desire to have her again made his blood boil. Her thighs slid across his lap, her hand stroking his erection as she leaned forward. The heat of her breath poured over him as her breasts pressed against his chest. He throbbed harder into her palm and her fingers tightened on his shaft in reply.

"If you're already tired, then let me handle it from here."

Her lips were hot on his ears as she sucked on his earlobe. The kissing trailed down to his neck, and he inhaled deeply, humming in pleasure. His fingers gripped the top of the back rest, leaning his head to encourage her to keep going. The heat of her body atop him sent his senses into overdrive. Scent and touch had become electrifying, adding to his building frenzy. Rocking his hips, he pressed his cock against the heat of her stroking hand.

The smell of her made him purr, taking it in and holding it. Heart racing, the tickling of her hair added to the way her thumb circled the tip of his dick. She shuffled, pushing his cock under the wet heat of her pussy, and sat slowly. He slid inside, her body tightening in greeting. She let out a moan, and he reached to kiss her neck, the urge to nibble and drink rattling his core.

"Not yet." Her voice was sultry as she shoved him back in place. "I'm in charge."

She bit his neck, nibbling. "Ouch. What was that for?"

"I thought that's what you're into now." Brushing her hair to one shoulder, she pointed at the fang marks.

Jakob licked his lips. "Careful. You do make me hungry."

Collapsing back into him, she nibbled his neck once more. He shifted, pushing his pelvis up to ride deeper inside her. Her teeth abandoned their play, moaning into his neck. Clara ground against him, arching back with her hands pressing down on his chest. Blue eyes glared down at him, holding him prisoner. Hot and tight, his cock throbbed inside her wet heat while her body rocked atop him, her breast swaying.

Each tilt of her hips made him grip the couch tighter. The wood creaked and cracked under the pressure. Claws popped through the leather. Jakob's body came alive, but he willed himself to indulge the swaying goddess on his lap. Fangs ached, a want for blood creeping forward. His eyes shifted to the bite mark and the flavor still fresh on his mind made him growl with want.

Clara's hand lifted, gripping his throat, demanding he meet her eyes. "Not yet."

She shifted and her pussy tightened on him. His breath caught, her pace changing, more aggressive. Fingers tightened on his throat, and he clawed into the leather. The growling grew in his chest. Her other hand trailed like searing wax trickling down his torso. He throbbed inside her, and she clamped tight, gasping. His eyes went to chase her hand to her pussy, and she leaned in, choking him. Wild and enthralled, his golden stare returned to the blue eyes. Her body gripping his cock tight, rubbing, and stroking his entire length.

"I want you to watch me come."

Jakob licked his lips, her body tensing, lifting and grinding down on him ever faster as she moaned. Her breath quickened. He could smell the rise of a coming orgasm. His claws slicing through the leather, balling into a fist on the shreds, fighting his want to feed on her, to overpower her.

"Are you hungry?"

His body tensed under her, and she smirked, slowing her rocking. A cold wake hit his neck where she had kept him at bay. Every muscle twitched in his body, fighting the desire to lunge forward, to sink his fangs into her so he may have another sampling of the sweet red nectar within her. Clara leaned back, her hands bracing against his knees. He took in her body, the plump breasts, the way her waist dipped just enough to break away into curvy hips. Her body throbbed around his dick, reminding him she had brought them to the edge of coming only to abandon it with reckless desire.

"Touch me," she commanded.

He released the leather tatters, his clawed hands gentle as they gripped her hips. Sliding her forward, he realigned with her, his cock diving deep again. She moaned and rocked slowly. Jakob licked a fang as his hands wandered up her body to grip her breasts. She tightened, and he responded by pinching her nipples. Her breath caught, and he twisted them, earning him a shriek. Again, her body throbbed around his dick, and it excited him to feel her react to him at every level. His hands snaked over her ribs and wrapped the arch in her back.

Caving to his hunger, he opened his jaws wide, fangs flashing. Clara rocked forward, her nails digging into his lower jaw, slamming him back. A growl escaped his lips, vibrating through her.

Her lips hovered above his, eyes searching as he hissed. "I didn't say you could eat," she warned.

His jaw ached from the hold. A shudder of rising arousal rolled through him. "I'm starving," he protested.

Grinding against him, her other hand slid between them. Fingers pressed against the base of his shaft, slick with her honey, curious to feel how he slid in and out of her. He gripped her ass cheeks, thrusting angry and hard against her. Her lips pressed firm onto his, breasts hot on his skin. Powerful strokes made her hum into his mouth, their tongues rubbing and diving, lapping out for one another. She caught his between her teeth and earned another growl from him. Her fingers between them tightened, demanding he keep going.

Pulling away, she leaned back, her grip on his jaw falling away. She went back to rocking on him, her nipples bouncing from the efforts of his pounding. Little yelps escaped her, his cock hard and engorged. Her eyebrows lifted high.

"Don't you dare come. I didn't say you could, Jakob."

Grunting, he slowed, agonized to fill her, to have her take it into her body and cry out into the night.

"Am I allowed to do anything?" he whined, his voice deepened, frustrated.

She smirked, sitting still, and pushing his hands from her. "You may taste me."

Biting her lip, she raised an eyebrow. Her heartbeat fluttered at her own words. She tensed, rising to her feet, leaving his throbbing erection to the cold air. The shine showed her dripping thighs; her body elated to have him inside her. Jakob licked his lips, his eyes lingering on her pussy.

Why does it smell like peaches? And I just feel... thirsty for them, for her, for the honey her body is pouring forth for me and only me.

15

Sweet Release

Clara's body shook in anticipation. Jakob looked monstrous and ravenous. Yet, she had kept him in place, and he had allowed her to take charge, folding to her every whim and desire. On any day, he could overpower her, his animalistic instinct filling with the undying need to fuck and feed. His end game would be to taste her blood, but only if she allowed it. It scared her, and yet, she couldn't deny how much how much she wanted to feel his fangs on her neck, piercing her skin.

He stood, rising slowly as he towered over her. Her heart skipped a beat, her chest aching. A silken tongue licked the wound there, laying a tender kiss. She closed her eyes, letting his hands travel down her cheeks, stroking her hair. Another stroke of his tongue, wet against the fang marks and again, a tender kiss. Enthralled with his touch, she did nothing, standing still so he may *taste her* as promised.

The suckling kisses flowed downward, leaving a burning trail over her collarbone, between her breasts, and through the center of her torso. Then hovered above her bellybutton. The heat of his kisses, his breath made her swollen pussy ache, and she could feel herself growing wet once more. The anticipation. Then his hands glided down her hips, cupping her ass cheeks as Jakob shouldered between her thighs, kneeling before her, taking one leg over.

"Swallow me up, Jakob." And there it was. The echo of their past he had longed to hear, goading him.

He glared at her with those slitted golden eyes. She balanced herself, a hand on his free shoulder. A wave of yearning filled her, her other hand gripping her breast. His lips pressed into her folds, capturing her clit and her leg buckled in response, but he wrapped his arms around, anchoring his meal from moving. He twisted, letting the cold of the leather loveseat add to the sensory overload unfolding between her thighs. And she screamed and screamed, and it only made him suck harder, longer, intertwining their passion.

Both of her hands clawed on the top of his head, fighting the sensations to push and pull him into her pussy. A numbing pleasure wracked her body. Each leg laid over a heavily muscled shoulder. They shook with the orgasm exploding from her. Another cry into the night did nothing to quell how deeply he drank from her. His tongue rolled across and flicked her jewel and she arched.

Failing to let her catch her breath, Jakob's tongue slid inside her; her eyes rolled back, legs shuddering as she pulled his face into her. A purr rolled from him, adding to the unfolding orgasm. His lips wrapped around her clit and his fingers slipped inside, thrusting to keep her at the peak of pleasure. A primal scream filled the room as she squeezed around them, ecstasy electrifying her body, her mind lost to passion.

Jakob abandoned his suckling.

He kissed and licked her inner thigh. His stroking fingers aggressively riding a sweet spot that took her breath away. His fangs popped through her skin. Her hands reached to brace herself on the couch as he ate her offering. With each gulp and suck on her inner thigh, she throbbed against his stroking fingers. He released his bite and licked the wound he'd inflicted.

Clara gasped for air, overwhelmed, as he abandoned her quivering legs and stood. He towered over her, his presence dominating.

"Fuck me," she commanded.

His hands rode up her thighs while his hard cock slid inside her wet pussy. They moaned as he braced himself on the loveseat. She arched into him, her ass cheeks barely teetering on the edge only kept in place by the fast-paced pounding. He grew harder with each knock of their hips, his purring transitioning to moaning. Leather ripped and shredded where he clung to the couch. Her hands were lost, fluttering, and searching where to hold onto him. They pulled on his arms, his waist, and his back and repeated the desperation of keeping him in and on top of her.

"Come on top of me!"

Another moan escaped him. He pulled out, rubbing his throbbing cock. She arched, giving him the full canvas of flesh to paint. Hot cum squirted across her stomach and breasts. She rubbed it across her skin, smitten by his need to follow her every whim despite looking so monstrous.

"Again. I want to watch you come again."

A growl was his answer, and his hardened length returned inside her. She orgasmed, yet again, peaking as her body shook in a wave of exhilaration. Through heavy, lidded eyes, she stared into his golden glare. All he saw, all he felt, all he wanted was her. He would devour her in more than one way, and she wanted it, gave herself up to it. Another moan and grunt came from him. Again, he abandoned her body and ejaculated across the canvas. She hummed, arching to greet the hot liquid once more. He knelt, fangs pressing through the wound they had created moments before. He drank from her and to her surprise, she peaked again. Her breath caught and she lunged forward. His fingers pressed inside her, and she wailed from the orgasmic sensation. Her fingers clawed his back and shoulder, her body shuddering with pleasure.

At last, he released, rocking back to sit on the floor and releasing her to melt into the couch. Both panted, their skin glistening in the low light of the rising sun. He stared at her in disbelief, and she grinned, a shudder rolling through her.

"You okay?" He leaned back on his arms, the couch in tatters from his claws. "Sorry, I ruined the couch."

She laughed, swallowing. "It's not mine."

He laughed. "Aren't you going to be in a heap of trouble over that?"

She smirked. "He said I couldn't steal or destroy it. Not my fault he kept it in a broken home and a wild animal tore it to hell."

Jakob collapsed onto his back. She pulled herself from the couch. Before he could protest, she straddled him, capturing his still hard erection back into the warmth of her pussy. She rocked on him, playing with herself. His body ached. He had spent the whole time doing everything in his power not to shift, not to become the Chupacabra. He had clawed into the couch, sucked her blood to take the edge off, and Clara had taken care of the lustful whims. Even when his mind hit a point of scattered thoughts, she had taken charge, rode him like a rider on a bull with one hand on his neck.

He tilted back, enjoying the building waves he knew would soon tighten, encircling him as she peaked. Again, her fingers wiggled between where they connected, wanting to feel him move in and out of her. He reached up, gripping her breasts and she moaned. Her pace sped up, more aggressively as the throbbing inside her escalated. She arched, leaned into his hands as he twisted her nipples. Her eyes cracked open, meeting his stare. He licked his lips.

"You could kill a man with a libido like that," he muttered, marveling over her unapologetic enjoyment of his body.

She grinned, on the edge of an orgasm. "But you're no man."

His hands fell away, pulling her down to him, his breath hot on her neck. "You're right."

Wrapping his arms around her, squeezing her firm, he thrust hard and fast. She screamed, wiggling like an animal in his grasp. He could feel the wet rush soaking them both as she came hard and unforgiving. Another shriek, and he kept going, making her ride out her hardest orgasm, torturing her until her voice finally broke. He rolled her over, hovering over her as she throbbed. Pressing his lips onto her, he ground slowly until he too began to moan. Once more, he left her pussy, rubbing his hard cock and painted her body. She panted, goosebumps drifting across her skin.

He lay beside her, catching his breath. "I can't."

Swallowing, she laughed. "Me neither. How the hell did you rebound like that?"

"That's a three-day advantage I get once a month," he snorted. "I could ask you how the hell you came that much and wanted more."

"Getting off on your cock only makes me want to go, again and again."

He looked at her. "I think that's the best compliment I've ever gotten."

She laughed and rolled up to her feet. "I need a shower."

"Shit." Jakob covered his face. "I need to fix your bathroom!"

Clara nudged his leg. "Upstairs works fine. I'll get the water going, takes a whole five minutes for the hot water to start anyhow. You going to join me?"

Jakob inhaled deeply, "Yeah, I'll be up once I catch my breath."

She laughed at the remark. He watched as her body sashayed up the stairs. Looking back to the destroyed antique loveseat, he grinned. One last *fuck you* to the asshole who had taken everything from him. He had it all back. Clara and the property. He didn't care if it had been his at some point, only that he could restore the rotting estate back to its former glory, to honor the stories his mother told of their ancestors and the Chupacabra.

Bing! He blinked, looking up at the cracked popcorn ceiling, brown with water stains. Rolling to his side, he reached for his pants and slid them over. Diving into the pockets, he found two cell phones. First was Clara's.

[MotherFuckingDick: You can keep the couch.]

Jakob furrowed his brow, glancing at the tattered thing and laughed. He then grabbed his own to see voicemails from his father. Sighing, he stood on his feet and climbed the stairs as he listened. His dad sounded panicked, unsettled, and rushed as he spoke.

"Jakob, you need to be careful. I just got off the phone with a Doc Samson. He apparently knew your mother, was her doctor of sorts and... look, he's a local vet in your town. Go see him. It's too dangerous to talk about over the phone. He can help. He said if you don't settle down soon, you won't be able to shift back. JR, be careful."

The message ended. Jakob could hear the shower going. The sound of the curtain sliding and the creaking of a body stepping into a clawfoot tub, letting him know Clara had started to wash herself. He pulled up Doc Samson's cell phone number. He aimed to call, and thought better of it, afraid Clara would overhear. He texted the old man:

[Jakob: Hey, my old man said you could help me out with my condition.]

"Jakob, the water is hot," Clara called out in a sing-song voice.

He smirked and announced, "The Mother Fucking Dick said you can keep the couch."

His phone buzzed. "Why would he change his mind?"

"Hell, if I know. Be in there in just a minute. Need to charge my phone." He walked away from the bathroom door, following her scent into the room she had been staying in.

[Doc Samson: Please tell me Clara is with you.]

Jakob scratched his chest, weighing the question.

[Jakob: Yeah. Why does that matter?]

[Doc Samson: You'll need someone to keep you human.]

[Jakob: What the fuck does that mean??!!]

[Doc Samson: It's either you get stuck in a shift, or you fuck the beast out of you, son. If you're hungry, come see me. I have anything you could want. Free buffet.]

Jakob hung his head in defeat.

[Jakob: Does this whole damn town know?]

There was a delay before...

[Doc Samson: We've always known ;)]

Epilogue

*G*eorge Worcestershire paled. To spite Clara, he had installed a hidden camera, but he never imagined it would return to haunt him. When Suzie had revealed Jakob Regadera had become town sheriff, he had changed his mind on making an unannounced visit. Instead, he had sent Sharon, not realizing she'd have the gall to brag about their sexual relationship while he was still married.

In short, the town gossiper ate her alive and sent her back to him.

Bile burned in his throat as he glared at the video playing on the screen. Physical proof that Jakob was indeed a monster. Swallowing, he hit rewind and pushed play. Glowing eyes, shiny patches of scales. As Jakob fucked his ex-wife, George pushed pause. He never got that face from her, never allowed her to be the dominant one in the bedroom in the ten years they were married.

He pushed play, watching as fangs flashed, then paused it again.

"Did you know this whole time he was a monster, Clara?" he muttered, judging her calm expression, a hand reaching for Jakob's throat.

Again, he pushed play, fast forwarding as Jakob shredded the couch and Clara knelt before him. Panic rattled through him. He exited the video. With a drag and drop, it was in the virtual trash can. Right clicking, he hovered over the *empty trash can* command.

"What good is this to me?" Lost in his anger, his face turned red. "I caught the damn Chupacabra on tape..." He bit his lip, blood trickling down. "I caught my wife cuddling with Chupacabra after fucking him on my damn couch."

With a click, the file ceased to exist.

The End

Honey Cummings

A passionate, award-winning author of Fantasy, Honey has turned her aim toward erotica. Blending everyday scenarios, and crafting them into steamy, blood-boiling moments for every shade of audience. Whether you want something short and hot, like a student-teacher hook up to the more paranormal flair, where Sleep with Sasquatch has unexpected bonus, look forward to erotic short stories, novellas, and hopefully a Trilogy in the future. Honey's debut erotic short landed at No. 3 in Urban Erotica and continues to satisfy readers time and time again. Be sure to leave her a review and let her know what you think!

amazon.com/Honey-Cummings/e/B07WFX5FDX
AuthorHoneyCummings.com
instagram.com/authorhoneycummings
twitter.com/HoneyCummings2
facebook.com/
Author-Honey-Cummings-101408818012749

MORE HONEY CUMMINGS BOOKS

Sleeping with Sasquatch
Cuddling with Chupacabra
Naked with New Jersey Devil
The Erotic Cryptid Collection

Laying with the Lady in Blue
Wanton Woman in White
Beating it with Bloody Mary
The Erotic Ghosts Collection

Beau and Professor Bestialora
The Goat's Gruff
Goldie and Her Three Beards
Pied Piper's Pipe
Princess Pea's Bed
Pinocchio and the Blow Up Doll
Jack's Beanstalk
Pulling Rapunzel's Hair
The Urban Erotica Fairy Tale
Collection

Curses & Crushes: KU short story

Queen's Incubus: YONDER webnovel

WRITING AS VALERIE WILLIS

Cedric: The Demonic Knight
Romasanta: Father of Werewolves
The Oracle: Keeper of the Gaea's Gate
Artemis: Eye of Gaea
King Incubus: A New Reign
Queen Succubus: Holder of the Crown

Val's House of Musings: A Mixed Genre Short Story Collection

Writer's Bane: Research 101
Writer's Bane: Formatting

WRITING MM ROMANCE AS VC WILLIS

The Prince's Priest
The Priest's Assassin
The Assassin's Saint

The Champion's Lord: YONDER webnovel
Champion's Love: KU short story

MORE BOOKS FROM 4 HORSEMEN PUBLICATIONS

EROTICA

ALI WHIPPE
Office Hours
Tutoring Center
Athletics
Extra Credit
Financial Aid
Bound for Release
Fetish Circuit
Now You See Me
Sexual Playground
Swingers
Discovered
XTC College Series Collection

ARIA SKYLAR
Twisted Eros
Seducing Dionysus

CHASTITY VELDT
Molly in Milwaukee
Irene in Indianapolis
Lydia in Louisville
Natasha in Nashville
Alyssa in Atlanta
Betty in Birmingham
Carrie on Campus
Jackie in Jacksonville
A Humorous Erotica Collection

DALIA LANCE
My Home on Whore Island
Slumming It on Slut Street
Training of the Tramp
The Imperfect Perfection
Spring Break
72% Match
It Was Meant To Be... Or Whatever

NICK SAVAGE
The Fairlane Incidents
The Fortunate Finn Fairlane
The Fragile Finn Fairlane
The Complete Package

LGBT Erotica

Dominic N. Ashen
Steel & Thunder
Storms & Sacrifice
Secrets & Spires
Arenas & Monsters
My Three Orc Dads: a Novella
Before the Storm: a Novella

Eskay Kabba
Hidden Love
Not So Hidden
Signs of Affection
Deeply Devoted to Him
Honest Love
A Plane and Simple Connection

Grayson Ace
How I Got Here
First Year Out of the Closet
You're Only a Top?
You're Only a Bottom?
I Think I'm a Serial Swiper
Lookin in All the Wrong Places
What Makes Me a Whore?
A Breach in Confidentiality
Back Door Pass
My European Adventure
An Unexpected Affair
Finding True Love
The Dr. Cage Chronicles

Leo Sparx
Before Alexander
Claiming Alexander
Taming Alexander
Saving Alexander
The Fall of the House of Otter
The Case of Armando

Robert Lewis
Someone to Love
Someone to Come Home To
Someone to Kiss

Discover more at
4HorsemenPublications.com